THE WINDS OF CHANGE

THE WINDS OF CHANGE

Carmel Birkmyre

ATHENA PRESS
LONDON

THE WINDS OF CHANGE
Copyright © Carmel Birkmyre 2006

All Rights Reserved

No part of this book may be reproduced in any form
by photocopying or by any electronic or mechanical means,
including information storage or retrieval systems,
without permission in writing from both the copyright
owner and the publisher of this book.

ISBN 1 84401 317 0

First Published 2006 by
ATHENA PRESS
Queen's House, 2 Holly Road
Twickenham, TW1 4EG
United Kingdom

Printed for Athena Press

In memory of my wonderful parents, John and Pat.

Acknowledgements

Thanks for the support over the years from my five sisters and four brothers: Anne, Mike, Fran, Steve, Bernard, Mary, Vinnie, Clare and Cathy.

Thanks also to my husband Ian and my two sons, Martin and Simon, for their part in helping me to get this story together.

Thanks to Gaynor for being such a wonderful friend for the past twenty years.

Many thanks too to Bob and Joan for their support over the years.

I hope life is kind to you all and true happiness is yours.

Carmel

Sarah climbed the stone steps, feeling vulnerable and uncertain of what the future held for her. She was far away from home and her family; home was a small village outside Leeds in Yorkshire. It had not been the easiest of childhoods for her, as the second of five children.

Her father was a miner at the local colliery, and Mother took in washing. Times were very hard, so she tried to contribute financially as well as running the house.

It was wartime and everything was in short supply, but Sarah's parents did their best to see that there was always food on the table. They were good, loving parents; honest and hard working, full of "true Yorkshire grit".

Sarah's two brothers and two sisters all showed strong determination, a strong inherited trait from their parents; a strength of character enabling them to survive in the hard world in which they found themselves.

For some time Sarah had expressed a desire to go into service, but her father had not wanted her to, it was not really the way he wanted his daughter to earn a living. He said it was "pampering to the whims of the hoity-toity"! Father was a plain, down-to-earth kind of person with very simple needs, and he did not feel that Sarah should be a "glorified servant".

However, after much persuasion and a promise to write at least once a week, Sarah set off on her journey towards a new job. She had secured a position as a parlour maid for Lord and Lady Chandler, in London.

Her future awaited her in this vast, impersonal city. With a few belongings in an old suitcase that had been in the family for more years than she cared to remember, Sarah boarded the train with very mixed feelings. She would miss her family terribly, but she kept trying to think ahead and be positive.

Her mother had packed some lunch for her journey; she could still see her mother's face, tear-stained but still trying to smile, with her soft, white lace handkerchief crumpled in her hand.

They had said their goodbyes at the house. Father had driven her to the station and wished her well, saying that if she was not happy she could always come home again, and to keep in touch.

Sarah's sisters Alice and Brenda, had made her a cake; chocolate, her favourite. The boys, Edmund and Gregory, had put together a wonderful wooden trinket box for her, as a token of how much she would be missed by everyone. They had also put some photographs of all the family in it. They were a family with very few material things; but they valued each other greatly. Mother had also provided a gift of two lace petticoats that she had made herself.

Sarah knocked on the huge wooden door, and the brass knocker seemed to make an echoing sound. Quite a while afterwards a smartly dressed man answered the door; she was later to find out that he was the "head butler".

She was brought into an enormous room where she was told to wait for the mistress of the house. The room was magnificent, Sarah had never seen such lavishness in her life, with its rich, deep velvet drapes and a large crystal chandelier hung from an elaborately moulded ceiling.

So this was how wealthy people lived, such sophistication and extravagance! Her eyes stopped on a splendid piano in one corner of the room with a set of silver candelabras on top of it, and a small mahogany stool with several sheets of music spread across it. There was no doubt that the people who enjoyed the comfort of this room had style and elegance.

Just then the door slowly opened and in walked the most charming lady that Sarah had ever seen. This was the lady of the house. She introduced herself as Lady Chandler. Her dress was beautiful, in emerald green velvet, with cream lace and a mother of pearl necklace. She had long auburn hair swept up. Sarah found herself staring at her then, realising she was doing so, tried very hard to look elsewhere.

"I trust that you had a good journey?" Lady Chandler said. "I expect you would like to see the servants' quarters and get settled in? Blake will show you your room and after you have bathed and changed, dinner will be ready below stairs."

She was extremely polite – what Sarah would have called "a real lady to her fingertips", with a wonderfully quiet air of authority about her.

But Sarah was instantly made to realise her position in the household. Her place was "below stairs". Even though Sarah knew that her life and her mistress's were poles apart, she still felt that her new employer seemed a warm, approachable person.

Blake was the gentleman she had seen earlier. He struck her as a strict, disciplined person who in his capacity as head of all the household servants expected high standards in all household duties undertaken. She felt sure that she would give of her best, as her mother had always shown them a very hard-working example.

Everything seemed so still and quiet in her room later. There was a small white porcelain vase on an oak chest of drawers with fresh cut flowers in it. The scent from them filled the room, and with the sun streaming through an open window Sarah smiled to herself.

After running a bath containing lavender salts, and feeling quite refreshed after immersing in it, Sarah dried herself and changed, putting one of her new cotton petticoats on underneath a tartan dress, and made her way down to the kitchen.

As Sarah walked along the corridor and down the stairs she could smell freshly baked bread and cakes.

Opening the door to the kitchen, there was a sudden clatter like pans falling to the floor, and an angry voice shouted, "Damnation! what a day I am having!"

Sarah was almost afraid to enter the room, nervously she walked in.

"Who might you be, young lady?"

"Sarah Watkins, miss, the new parlour maid."

"Well now, come in. I am Mrs Travis, the cook. Pleased to meet you." She was a round, jolly looking person with short cropped hair and rosy cheeks. She poured Sarah some freshly made tea and offered her a buttered scone. They chatted generally about the weather and Sarah's family then a large clock struck on the mantelpiece four times; the cook rose from her seat and removed a roast chicken and potatoes from the oven. Showing Sarah where everything was she asked her to set the table ready for their meal. A lace tablecloth covered the kitchen table, just like the kind that Sarah had seen in the expensive high street shops in Leeds. She was told to set six places. As she placed the cutlery on the table the other servants began to come in. The meal was quite a formal affair with Blake at the head of the table; he carved the chicken and Jenny, the assistant to the cook, placed meat on the dinner plates. She was a young, fresh-faced girl of about twenty; a little younger than Sarah, who was twenty-two.

Jenny smiled at Sarah and nodded to her to pass the

plates round. Before they began their meal a simple prayer of thanksgiving was said by Blake, then Sarah was asked to stand up and was formally introduced to the other staff. Blake said that he hoped she would look upon them as her second family.

Veronica, Lady Chandler's personal maid, was polite but made it quite clear she thought herself a cut above the others.

In contrast, Henry, Lord Chandler's valet, was a much nicer person, with a good sense of humour, telling anyone who would listen little anecdotes.

Perhaps life at Swarbrick Manor might not be so bad after all. Sarah bid everyone a good night as she had an early start in the morning; six o'clock, her first day, and she wondered what lay in store for her, also what the master of the house would look like. Sarah lay in her bed, her thoughts keeping her awake, then sleep came and the next thing she was aware of was waking to the sound of someone knocking on her door.

Sarah put on her dressing gown and timidly unlocked the door. It was Jenny; she had come to tell Sarah it was five o'clock and it was time to get washed and changed for her duties. Jenny gave her a neatly pressed starched blue and white uniform and a white cotton cap and she was told that she was responsible for her own work clothes, and to make sure that they were always clean and pressed.

Putting on her clothes quickly Sarah tied up her hair, it almost reached her waist now, and she made her way down to the servants' room on the next landing where she was given cloths, polish and cleaning equipment.

Sarah was told by Blake to make a start in the "Primrose Room"; this room was part of the west wing of the house, which tended to be used more when the Chandlers had visitors to stay. But this morning Sarah had to clean this room because later that day there was going to be a meeting of the local parish committee in there, to discuss their latest agenda on fund-raising events. Lady Chandler had been a member of the committee for three years now, and she seemed to find it rewarding. It also took up quite a bit of her time, which she could do as she had no family to consider and plenty of time on her hands. She was unable to have children due to a bad horse riding accident in her youth. This subject was not mentioned, mainly because it still seemed to upset her, and she carried terrible feelings of guilt about it as a consequence.

Sarah thought that human nature could be cruel in dealing such a blow to someone like Lady Chandler, who was such a kind, sensitive person.

Lord Chandler was a very distinguished, business-like person, apparently "a self-made man", so they said. Sarah was introduced to him on her second day; he seemed to be friendly but was somewhat preoccupied. Sarah could not help noticing a certain look of sadness in his eyes.

He explained to Sarah that she would be on a month's trial, and if they found her work satisfactory she would become a permanent member of the staff. He asked her about her family and when she mentioned that she came from Leeds he seemed to take more interest; apparently he was born in Leeds and grew up just a few miles away from Sarah's home.

Then the telephone rang; he excused himself and left the room. Sarah finished cleaning various brass ornaments and then went to the servants' kitchen for tea. In some ways Sarah felt she had been at Swarbrick Manor a lot longer than a couple of days, and she seemed to be adjusting to her routine and new way of life. The following day was Sunday. Sarah had been given the afternoon off as a reward for her hard work.

She had decided to go the park nearby. The cook had put together some home-made sandwiches and lemonade for her.

Sarah sat down by the lake and watched the ducks and swans swimming by so gracefully; things seemed to be working out well for her; maybe when she got back later she would write to her family and tell them how she was getting on.

Later that day, the rain poured down outside her bedroom window as Sarah sat on her bed composing a letter to her parents. She thought how pleased they would be to know she was fairly happy and liking her work, and that her employers seemed to be kind and were taking care of their daughter.

Sarah's father still had his reservations about her decision but he was trying to come to terms with it and keep an open mind as he was beginning to realise that his daughter's independence was important to her and he was trying to respect that.

She didn't think at the moment she would mention the young gentleman she had become acquainted with in the park; they would only worry unnecessarily. He seemed quite nice, and apparently was a valet for another "well-to-do" family who lived across the park.

Edward was three years older than her with dark hair, warm brown eyes and the most wonderful smile. She laughed to herself; surely she couldn't be falling for him already, the idea was ridiculous! She brushed her long blonde hair and then put it into a plait. If she worked hard she would be kept on and her job was far more important than any silly romance!

Sarah was a practical, sensible girl with plenty of common sense, and like her mother she could turn her hand to most jobs. She sealed up her letter, put on her cloak and bonnet, and walked out to post it. On the way back down the street, she thought about how she would spend her first wage. When she had sent half of her money home to help the family, maybe she would go and buy material for a couple of new dresses...

Supper was beef broth; steaming hot and wholesome. Sarah sat and ate it thinking how lucky she felt with a good job, nutritious food and a room of her very own.

Lady Chandler had asked to see Sarah after her meal; she hoped it wasn't to do with her work. When she entered the room after knocking she must have looked a bit anxious as Lady Chandler said to her, "You needn't look so worried Sarah, I only wish to ask you if you would like to choose some wallpaper for your room."

Sarah's room was in need of redecorating, and Lord Chandler and Lady Chandler had mutual friends who owned a wallpaper factory. Mr and Mrs Carter would be able to recommend some suitable wall covering and supply it at a discount price.

Sarah was quite taken back by this and said, "Thank you Madam, that would be very nice."

Lady Chandler said that Blake would go with Sarah, as the Carters knew Blake. Sarah was excused and went up to her room, drew the curtains and got ready for bed; tomorrow she would go shopping for things for her own room, she could hardly believe it!

As she lay in bed, Sarah tried to imagine how her room would look, but she felt quite tired and drifted off quickly. She awoke to the sun shining brightly outside her window, and there was a message that had been slipped underneath her door, probably by Jenny, telling her to meet Blake promptly at nine thirty in the hallway at the main entrance of the house. Finding that she had two hours to spare before going out, Sarah decided to catch up on some more correspondence, including a letter to her brother Edmund who was presently serving with the Royal Air Force.

He always greatly looked forward to Sarah's letters, along with his special parcels from their mother. There wasn't anything of any great expense within them, but they were very much appreciated.

Sarah was particularly close to Edmund, and she thought that maybe she would confide in him about her gentleman friend, as she respected him, and his opinion, and she was very proud of him as he was serving his country. Sarah thought he was a brave, honest man.

As she wrote her letter, she couldn't help wondering whether Edmund had taken up with any lady friends, if he had much spare time. He had been sweet on a local girl before he went away to "join up", but as soon as he had gone she took up with the butcher's son, much to Sarah's disgust! Sarah though she might ask her employers' permission for Edmund to visit her one day on his next leave, it would be good to catch up on all the news with him.

Then Sarah remembered the promise she had made to her youngest sister, Alice, to write, and began to compose a letter to her. She told her that she had seen some very nice materials in a nearby store, and maybe she could make Alice one of those a-line skirts she wanted.

Although Alice was the youngest in their family, Sarah always thought of her as an old head on young shoulders. Far wiser than her sixteen years, Alice worked at the colliery with her father in a secretarial capacity, and on Sundays she sang in the local choir and made the evening meal to give Mother a night off. All in all she was very considerate, even though she was very career minded, far more than Sarah, she could still find time for her family, especially their parents.

In contrast, Brenda, who was older than Alice – by four years in fact – filled her head with movie star rubbish. She was happy to spend her days working in the local bakery and any evenings she could at the local picture house, watching all the latest films.

Brenda thought of herself as having a "forces sweetheart image", and played out the part to the full by walking out with lots of different gentlemen, which some of the family found amusing, except of course for Sarah's father who thought she should try to conduct herself more like Alice.

Alice, along with Sarah, was Father's favourite, simply because of their practical, sensible natures. He couldn't abide stupidity on any level, and didn't suffer fools gladly, as the saying goes. Although everyone loved him, Sarah often though her father was too set in his ways. He didn't adapt well to changes in his life and especially to Sarah moving away from the family home. What Sarah did appreciate, though, was the fact that her father really seemed to be trying hard to come to terms with it and trying to understand, which was quite difficult for him.

Sarah in so many ways was still his little blossom, as he called her. Allowances had to be made on both sides; she had come to realise that his manner and approach to things was only his way of showing her that he was concerned for her welfare, and deep down he had her best interests at heart.

She pictured him in his favourite armchair listening to the wireless, quietly smoking his pipe. The day he got the wireless it seemed to open up a whole new world for him, as he listened attentively to news of far-off countries; he could hardly spell some of their names, let alone visit them!

Mother got annoyed with him on several occasions; as she stood and tried to hold a conversation with him, maybe even of some importance, he would sit there, quite still, as if in his own world. And when she *did* finally get through to him, he would say, he was improving his mind. "Indeed!" Mother would say.

Sarah's parents were different in some ways, but in others they stood for the same values of honesty, family life and a strong belief that "hard work never killed anyone". That was definitely where she got her determination from; she wasn't one to give up on anything. And her mother had a very down-to-earth approach, which caused her to speak her mind on many occasions. Most of the family disliked this kind of "plain speaking", but she still told them exactly what she thought anyway.

Even so, Sarah still had a lot of admiration for her mother, as she knew, like her brothers and sisters, that her mother could have really made something of her life; she could have been a famous pianist, but her parents couldn't afford to encourage her ambition.

So Sarah's mother made the best of her life with Harry Watkins and worked hard with pride in herself, whatever simple tasks she was doing. Sarah was the same in that respect; "like mother like daughter". And whereas Sarah's father was reluctant for her to leave home and become independent, her mother, although she missed her, seemed to be encouraging her every step of the way.

Sarah loved her parents so, and felt that especially her mother worked too hard. She longed to give them a holiday by the seaside; she had heard that Brighton was very nice. Maybe in a while if she put some money by she would be able to treat them, if they would accept the offer.

She looked up at the clock on her bedroom wall. It was time to meet Blake. She mustn't keep him waiting; he was a stickler for punctuality. They arrived at the factory and were taken in by Mrs Carter, who gave them tea and biscuits in the office before showing them their stock.

Between them they decided upon a small floral print paper with a cream paint. Sarah thought that Lady Chandler would approve of their choice and the fact that they had kept the price down, as they had been instructed.

When they arrived back, it was a quick change and straight back to her duties; there was a dinner party that evening at the Manor, and the guests included some of the local gentry, also some of the members of the parish committee.

The cook was busy preparing for the dinner. There were to be four courses in all. Sarah had never seen such a huge amount of vegetables, fruit or food all together. Sarah had learnt from personal experience to keep well away from cook when she had to prepare for a dinner party! Pots and pans tended to get tossed around the kitchen.

Cook was a no-nonsense person, middle-aged, a round figured lady with a healthy complexion, and a hearty chuckle that could be heard halfway down the corridor.

Everyone was busy preparing the dinner table and the necessary seating arrangements. As the clock in the main hall struck eight the guests began to arrive; first of all the reverend Campbell, a middle-aged, portly man with a strong Scottish accent. His views on life were very outspoken.

Mr and Mrs Blackstock entered the hall next, a couple in their late thirties without children who were very much "career minded", especially since they had inherited Mrs Blackstock's father's mill. They were big hearted people who also gave generously to local worthy causes.

Mrs Blackstock helped out at one of the local hostels for the homeless, serving soup twice a week, while her husband attended to the maintenance side of the machinery in the business as he had always done manual work. She saw to the administration side of things as she had completed a secretarial business course, and she was also able to look after the books for the parish committee, which pleased everyone else no end as their interests lay in other areas.

Miss Featherstone had arrived with them this evening as she was having problems with her motor vehicle; she was a well-respected spinster of the parish who also was a schoolteacher in one of the nearby schools. She taught English and history and was in her late forties and had a lot in common with the Blackstocks, all being "Yorkshire people".

Mr Wood had started to come along to the parish meetings four weeks ago, after being asked to come by Miss Featherstone; they had talked previously of the committee's activities at school, as Mr Wood was the caretaker there. Tonight he had brought with him two bottles of his best home-made wine, rhubarb; it was the finest he had made so far, and at the end of the dinner he wished to show slides of the last ornithology expedition he was on, which the others had expressed an interest in. He thought it should round off the evening well, as he took off his cap and scarf and entered the dining room.

Last but not least, Mrs Wendall arrived a little after the others as she had to ask a neighbour to look after her two foster children, Timothy and Grace, aged twelve and ten years, who had been with her for two years and had been a great source of comfort to her when her dear husband Thomas, had passed away twelve months before.

Her only son, Gerard, was now in his thirties and lived in London, working for a large newspaper. She was very proud of him, and he supported her and the foster children very well indeed, visiting her once a month and making sure everything was well.

The meal got underway. Mrs Travis had once again excelled in the kitchen, and the air was filled with good conversation and delight at such a delicious meal. Then the next fund-raising option was discussed, a bridge evening with the proceeds to go to the local hospital; maybe they would have some supper thrown in and then they could charge a little more. This seemed to be the general opinion of the group; after all, it was going to a good cause.

Six months ago Ms Featherstone herself had had to go into hospital for a minor operation, and was more than satisfied with her treatment.

Lord Chandler, who usually said very little on these occasions, actually seemed full of ideas and even had a suggestion of his own. He wanted to try and organise a car rally from Leeds to London, ending up outside the Houses of Parliament; everyone entering had to pay a fee. The

The Winds of Change

money raised would pay for a day at the seaside for the children and staff of one of the local children's homes. The rest of the committee thought it was a splendid idea and decided it should take place in two weeks' time, weather permitting! Lord Chandler smiled to himself, and Lady Chandler nodded agreeably.

After Mr Woods' slide show the evening drew to a close, and everyone said their goodbyes till the next meeting and went into the night. Lord and Lady Chandler retired to their drawing room with a request for two small liqueurs to be taken up to them shortly. The servants started to clear the room and chatted quietly as they took pots and a tablecloth down to their quarters.

Sarah had been with the Chandlers for six months now, and was a well established member of the household. The following day was a Sunday, and Sarah had a day off so she had arranged to meet her gentleman friend in their favourite spot by the boating lake in the park. That was a convenient meeting place. She got herself ready and felt in very good spirits all in all. She walked along to the park with a spring in her step, thinking things were turning out well, and life was good.

Edward was waiting on the bench in his tweed jacket and matching cap. Sarah thought to herself how smartly dressed he always was and that he had been a very good friend to her, especially when she first came to Swarbrick Manor.

They had actually met in the park. She had dropped a package while walking on the green, and he had very kindly picked it up for her. As Sarah got closer, she could not help but notice the look of concern on Edward's face.

"What ever is wrong with you, Edward?" Sarah said.

"I have some news to tell you, I have been offered a position in Switzerland with my present employer," Edward said.

Sarah swallowed hard, and just for a matter of seconds

sat and looked at Edward. In truth she was completely taken aback by what he had told her! Their friendship had been good, and in some ways she valued it greatly and she had grown quite fond of him. She had become used to having him around.

"So have you come to any decision at all yet?" Sarah asked.

"Not yet, I wanted to ask your opinion first," Edward said nervously. He looked into her eyes as though he was searching for some kind of answer there.

Sarah found herself feeling a little uncomfortable and got up and suggested they have a stroll around the lake. "I have a week to make my decision, it is not going to be an easy one as I have been happy in my position here," Edward said.

"Well, take your time, I am sure you will come to decide what is right for you, and I can always write if you do go," Sarah replied.

Just at that moment Edward looked as though he was going to burst and Sarah was no fool; she knew that it was solely due to what she had said.

"Sarah, I need to ask you if you would do me the honour of being my wife, and we could have a new life together in Switzerland," Edward said.

Sarah looked at Edward. "Sorry I can't, I must go now—" And she ran right out of the park and kept on going until she was quite out of breath and had reached home again.

She opened the back door to the servants' quarters to find Mrs Travis the cook and Albert the gardener sharing a pot of tea. They looked up and saw the flustered expression on Sarah's face. "What's wrong with you, my girl?" Mrs Travis asked with a note of concern.

"Nothing!" Sarah snapped, going straight up to her room. She did not feel like talking to anyone at that moment. Sarah felt quite shocked at what Edward had asked her, and did not have the remotest idea that he was even contemplating such a thing! If he had been he never gave her any inclination to think so.

Sarah sat looking out of the window and wondering just how long Edward must have felt that way. Well, what exactly was she supposed to do now? She felt a little saddened at the thought that this incident would without a doubt affect their friendship.

There was a knock at the door; it was Jenny, the cook's assistant; she had been asked to see if Sarah was all right.

"Jenny, I have just received a proposal of marriage from my friend Edward, which I would rather you did not tell anyone about," Sarah said sharply.

"If you wish, Sarah, but gosh, how exciting! Whatever did you say to him?" replied Jenny.

"Jenny, I just could not consider marriage at the moment," Sarah said.

"How can you be so matter-of-fact about something of that nature?" Jenny asked.

Jenny could not understand Sarah at times, even though they got on reasonably well together. They obviously had very different ideas concerning romance. Whereas Sarah was more down to earth and practical about matters, Jenny differed somewhat; due to a very romantic nature, she often daydreamed about a fine beau sweeping her off her feet. She truly believed one day it would happen.

Sarah teased her terribly about it, saying it was all nonsense.

Jenny returned downstairs and Sarah went and asked permission to make a phone call to her brother at the RAF base. Sarah was put through to an officer, who brought Edmund to the phone.

"Are you OK Sarah? There is nothing wrong, pet, is there?" Edmund enquired.

"Oh Edmund, I am in a mess!" Sarah began to cry.

"Please tell me what is wrong?" Edmund pleaded with her.

"You remember I told you about my friend Edward? Well, today he proposed to me," Sarah said.

"Well, that sounds wonderful Sarah. Why are you so upset?" Edmund asked.

"Because it is not what I want at all, my job is going really well and I thought we were friends! I have no idea where this notion has come from," Sarah said with some regret.

"Oh my, so what are you going to say to the poor chap?" Edmund asked.

"I have already told him that I can't possibly marry him, but then I did a really silly thing. I ran away from him. He just caught me off guard, I suppose," Sarah said defensively.

"Well, Sarah Watkins, you will just have to apologise to him and hope you can still be friends. In the meantime I have a few days' leave starting on Thursday. Could I come to the Manor and have a day with you?" Edmund asked her.

"That would be grand Edmund, I will write and let you know and I could meet you at the station," Sarah added, beginning to cheer up a little.

"I have to go now, Sarah. Keep your chin up – it's not the end of the world, see you soon," Edmund said.

Sarah put the phone down and felt a bit better already; it was good to talk to her brother; he was always good with problems. She was glad that she had caught him as Sarah had forgotten that he was going on an exercise tomorrow for a couple of days. No doubt he would have lots to tell her when she saw him, and she would find out how he was getting on with his pilot training.

For the time being Sarah had decided to send a note to Edward, as she could not bear to face him at the moment and sometimes she was better equipped to express herself on paper; just now she was liable to get tongue-tied and her words would not come out properly at all. Sarah sat in her room at her desk. All she could hear was the shrill sound of birdsong outside her window.

She began to write:

My dearest Edward,

I don't know what you must think of me rushing off in such a way like that. Please forgive me, I sincerely hope that this will not affect our friendship, and that you will understand my actions in time.

Sarah

She felt a little better but still knew she would have to face Edward again at some point. She would cross that bridge when she came to it. In the meantime she would have to go downstairs and have some tea.

When Sarah entered the room it went perfectly silent, she forced a smile and sat in her usual seat. Then the conversations continued around her as they all ate their mutton broth.

After tea Sarah went to get herself ready as she had arranged to go to a local dance with Jenny, and they were both looking forward to it immensely. They had bought new dresses for the occasion and left with strict instructions from Blake to be back by eleven o'clock.

They entered the dance hall feeling a little apprehensive to say the least, but they soon realised as the evening went on that they had no reason to feel like that at all. There were plenty of men and women of their own age, and some a bit older. They seemed very friendly and the hall had a very welcoming atmosphere.

At the dance, they met two girls who were also in service like them; Sadie and Yvette were apparently regulars at the weekly dance. They seemed to be good company and full of fun. They all had plenty of stories to exchange during the course of the night, of their work in the different households. They were having so much fun, in between dancing and chatting, that they did not notice the time!

When they realised it was eleven thirty Sarah and Jenny said their goodbyes to their new friends and talked of returning the following week if they could manage it. Now they had to think of how they were going to get back into the Manor, without disturbing the rest of the household.

They quietly crept around to the back of the servants' quarters.

Sometimes Albert, the gardener, left his ladders out by the shed, but tonight of all nights they were locked away out of sight. Sarah offered to give Jenny a bunk up the drainpipe. As Jenny tried to climb up she managed to tear her dress, which caused them both to burst out laughing and trying to control it only made them worse.

"We will have to quieten down or we will never get in this way," Sarah whispered.

"OK, Miss bossy boots!" Jenny uttered. She seemed to be getting a better grip on the drainpipe and gaining height.

"Aren't you the clever one now?" Sarah said.

"I knew that I could do it!" Jenny called back confidently to Sarah.

At that moment Jenny lost her footing and fell to the ground. "My arm hurts, I can't move it!" Jenny cried out.

"Oh, what should I do, we are for it now, aren't we?" Sarah said anxiously. She knocked loudly on the back door. Blake came to it in his dressing gown and was very angry to be woken up and to learn that they had behaved so foolishly. Sarah explained about Jenny.

Blake got changed and drove Jenny to the hospital, after telling Sarah to retire and that he would deal with the matter properly in the morning. Sarah did not like the sound of that at all! She did not sleep well at all, and in the morning she found a message by her door – it was from Blake!

Sarah dressed hurriedly into her uniform, and as she

went down the stairs she wondered what was going to happen to her. A feeling of sheer dread came over her as she entered the drawing room nervously.

Blake told Sarah to sit down and handed her a small glass of sherry. It seemed a strange way of being told off! But when Sarah looked up at Blake's face, she did not see anger but instead there was a sympathetic look in his eyes.

"I am afraid that I have some very bad news for you, Sarah my dear, it's concerning your brother Edmund. I am afraid he died whilst on exercise."

Sarah just felt completely numb; everything was one big blur; her heart was pounding so hard it felt like it would burst at any moment. Blake looked helpless; he wasn't a man who dealt easily with displays of emotions. He stood awkwardly next to Sarah and explained that she would obviously not be expected to continue her duties under the circumstances.

Sarah returned to her room and collapsed on her bed. She cried until she thought her heart would break. Her eyes were stinging and sore. She would miss her brother so much. Sarah thought back to her last conversation with him about Edward and how they were going to get together for a good chat. Sarah had been so proud of him.

The next day Blake ran Sarah to the train station and wished her well on her journey back to her family for Edmund's funeral. Her mother, who was normally a tower of strength, stood in the doorway looking totally lost and her father just sat staring into thin air.

Sarah's other brother and sisters were so relieved to see her. Alice made a pot of tea and attempted to try and hold things together for them to get through such a distressing time.

The morning of the funeral condolences arrived from all quarters, including a very nice letter from Lady Chandler. Sarah's mother was quite taken back by this thoughtful gesture. Sarah and she sat and talked of how Edmund had died doing a job that he loved; it was all he ever wanted to do. Sarah sighed as she thought of how much she would miss him and how he had left a big gap in her life. There would be no more brotherly advice.

Her father came over to her and hugged her tightly, and with a voice filled with mixed emotion, he said, "Well, blossom, this is a mess, isn't it?" With that he sat down at the table and sobbed uncontrollably. Sarah had never seen her father show such emotion before. She put her arm around him but felt completely helpless, and then her father got up and went into the kitchen. Sarah stayed in the parlour quietly thinking, her mind full of thoughts of her childhood. In her mind Sarah could see Edmund playing on the hill at a game of rounders with his friends and how he used to tease her when she asked to play. There was no mistaking that there had been a special bond between them.

Somehow they all managed to struggle through the funeral service; they had prepared a buffet for afterwards. It was plain and simple, as Edmund would have wished.

Sarah walked towards the church door to go outside and found to her surprise that her mother was deep in conversation with Lord Chandler of all people! Sarah certainly hadn't expected him to attend her brother's funeral! She got closer and could hear the conversation between her mother and Lord Chandler.

"...Vernon, you shouldn't have come here, Harry must never find out about Edmund, it would break him in. Lord Chandler took hold of Sarah's mother's hand, and with tears in his eyes he said, "Helen, I had to come, I am so sorry. It is still as we agreed; no one else knows that Edmund was my son – not even Eleanor! And it was the least that I could do, finding a position for Sarah to help you all out, seeing as you wouldn't let me help in any other way," Lord Chandler said defensively.

"We did appreciate that, as Sarah seemed so set on service work, and of course she has no idea that she didn't obtain the position on her own merit..."

They stood trying to comfort one another as Sarah hid out of sight behind a nearby tree. She felt as though she couldn't move. She was so angry! Her mother had always said that when you listened to other people's conversation, you never heard any good. She was so right! What on earth was Sarah going to do now?

The tears streamed down her face; she felt upset and extremely angry that between them her mother and Lord Chandler they had managed to manipulate her life in this way and also keep such a secret from them all. They obviously had their reasons, but all the same Sarah still felt an awful sense of betrayal.

And her poor father had loved Edmund so much, never realising that he wasn't his true son. How could her mother do such a thing to him? The question was, what was Sarah going to do now? She felt quite sick! She could ignore it all, and pretend she had never heard any of it... But whom was she trying to kid? Her conscience would not possibly allow her to do that, she couldn't live with herself. She knew exactly what she must do, but Sarah had to get her mother on her own first and ask her for herself.

They all made their way back to the house, where Lord Chandler maintained he had come to pay his respects as Sarah's employer. He left shortly after to return to the Manor. Sarah hid behind her grief, and couldn't even bear to look at him as he left.

The table in front of her was filled with sandwiches and pies, sherry for the ladies and beer for the gents. Sarah wasn't normally a drinker at all; she had on occasions seen the foolish actions of many people partaking of it, and that had been enough for her. But under the circumstances Sarah thought she would just have a small sherry – after all, she had received a terrible shock to her system. One thing was for certain; her feelings remained the same for Edmund. He had been one of the best brothers that a girl could wish for.

Sarah sat sipping her sherry and staring at her mother. She couldn't believe that she could carry on as normal. She wanted to shout out loud and tell her mother how angry she felt. Instead she sat and felt all the anger burning up inside her.

When their friends had gone home and things began to quieten down a little, Sarah's mother came over to her and asked if she was all right. Sarah wasn't all right – not one bit – and furthermore, she had no intentions of returning to her position after such deceit had taken place! Sarah went to stand up and slumped back down in the chair again. She was feeling the shock and the effects of three glasses of sherry.

Her mother said, "Sarah, I don't think that's the answer, drinking like that."

"Don't you, Mother? Well, that's a shame isn't it?" Sarah snapped.

"Don't talk to your mother like that, under this roof!" her father shouted.

"Dad, you don't know the half of it," Sarah replied.

"What is that supposed to mean my girl?" her father demanded "I think maybe you need to go and lie down for a while, they will need you back at work in a day or two," Father added.

"I don't intend to return to such a place and work for people who tell such lies!" Sarah said.

"What do you mean, Sarah? Have they mistreated you in some way, love?" her father asked with concern.

"Not exactly, but I no longer have the respect I had for them. Mother, I need to talk to you, and I don't feel very well," Sarah said.

"I am not surprised, Sarah. Come on, I will help you upstairs," her mother replied.

When they reached Sarah's bedroom door Sarah and her mother looked at one another. The door was shut and Sarah fell onto the bed and glared at her mother. She had always looked up to her mother and admired her most of all for her honesty. And now at the age of twenty-two to find out she had lied to all of them for all these years; Sarah couldn't bear it at all!

"Why, Mum? I know about Edmund and Lord Chandler being his real father, I heard everything in the graveyard," Sarah said sobbing.

"I am so very sorry, Sarah, it was such a long time ago it was for the best, Vernon and I belonged to two different worlds," her mother said.

"So you both decided to deceive my father! I find that so unfair," Sarah shouted.

"Sarah, I would rather you didn't speak to me that way, and it wasn't you in the situation; your father was far more reliable than Vernon. And we would have never been allowed to marry; his family had more social standing than mine," her mother said with regret.

"I just can't believe that you could do such a thing, Mother, you always taught us to be honest and upright!" Sarah said.

"You will never know, Sarah, how many times I longed to tell your father, but then I would see that look of pride in his eyes as he read one of Edmund's letters. He couldn't have cared more, or been more proud of him, like he is of all of you," Mother said.

"So what are you going to do now that Edmund is gone?" Sarah asked.

"Let sleeping dogs lie, I should think, don't you Sarah?" her mother replied.

"I'm not sure, Mum, I don't feel happy about this at all," Sarah retorted.

Just then there was a knock on the door; it was her father. "What are you two talking about then, is everything all right?" he asked.

Sarah said, "Do you mind if I have a rest now? I feel so tired. I will see you later."

"I will talk to you after, blossom, when you're feeling better," her father said quietly.

Her parents went downstairs and Sarah was left alone, feeling hurt and confused. It was the worst position she had ever been in, and oh how she wished she had never heard that conversation; then she would have been none the wiser!

Sarah awoke some time later, dizzy when she sat up on the bed. She felt terrible and looked it as she glanced in the dressing table mirror.

Her eyes were red and sore and she didn't know whether she was going to be sick or not. The clock in her room struck four; she must have slept for a couple of hours. Sarah was reluctant to go downstairs, as she felt rather ashamed of herself. Everything came flooding back to her and she felt the horror of it all. She would definitely steer clear of the sherry in future! It had not agreed with her at all; her head was pounding. When Sarah opened the parlour door there was only her father wiping his eyes with his hankie.

She went up and gave him a kiss on the top of his head as she always did.

"Now are you going to tell me what that was all about before, with your mother?" he asked.

"Where is Mother?" Sarah enquired, trying to play for time, as this was one conversation she definitely didn't want to have at all.

"She's gone out for a walk, she wanted some fresh air," her father said.

"I am sorry about before, Father, I had some sherry – a

bit too much – and I wasn't myself," Sarah replied.

A broad grin came over her father's face. "If you can't handle it, pet, you shouldn't have it then," he said laughing.

"I know, but I was just so upset, Father. We all had a very nasty shock, and they say it's good for that, don't they?" Sarah added.

"Well, that's one excuse isn't it, missy?" he said jokingly. Sarah's father smiled and put his arm around her. "Let's get you a butty and a nice cup of tea, that always helps."

Sarah loved her father so much; you could say she was "Dad's Girl" in every sense of the word, and although Sarah wouldn't always admit it, she had definitely inherited his stubbornness.

"Oh, by the way, Sarah, before I forget there was a gentleman on the phone for you when you were resting, I think he said he was called Edward, your mother spoke to him."

"Did he? I expect he wanted to say goodbye as he has to go away shortly overseas," Sarah said.

"Oh really? And where did you meet him, my girl? You've never mentioned him before!" her father said.

"I meant to, honestly Father. He really is a fine man. I met him in the park one day, he is a valet for a family near to Swarbrick Manor," Sarah said defensively.

"Well anyway, he said that he would call again at seven. And when do you have to return to work, Sarah?" her father asked.

"Oh, I am not sure at the moment. I will try and phone Lord Chandler tomorrow," Sarah replied.

The next day was Monday, and if Sarah's memory served her correctly, Edward would have to leave on Tuesday. That was another awkward situation that Sarah would have to face up to, but at least she hoped she had softened the blow by writing that letter to him.

The back door opened and in walked Mother, anxiously looking in Sarah's direction for any form of reaction.

"Are you having a cuppa with us, Mother? And there are plenty of sandwiches left," Sarah said.

"I will just have a cup of tea for now," Mother said quietly.

They sat and no one really knew what to say at that moment. The silence was becoming a little uncomfortable, then the phone rang. Sarah answered it, half expecting Edward's voice. Instead it was Lady Chandler, enquiring after the family and expressing her condolences. It was obvious to Sarah that she had no idea of what Sarah now knew; either that or she was putting on a very convincing act. She said that Sarah could return to work on Thursday; Sarah hesitated then thanked her and put the receiver down.

Now she felt angry again; Sarah didn't really want to thank her. Everything had gone wrong. She wanted to say that she was never going to go back there again. But if Lady Chandler really didn't have any idea, which Sarah suspected she didn't, then it wasn't fair to take things out on her, as she was such a wonderful, warm and kind person, and faultless as an employer.

Just then the phone rang again, and this time it *was* Edward, right on time. He always was punctual and had been a good friend to her, every bit as much as Edmund, only in a different way.

Before she spoke, Sarah thought of poor Edmund and how she would miss him. She couldn't help wondering what Edmund would have made of all this, and if he had known Lord Chandler was his real father, would he have acknowledged him at all?

Sarah would never know that now, but one thing she did know about Edmund was that he had possessed a good heart and was a very forgiving person. Sarah knew this only too well from the rare occasions when they had disagreed about certain things.

"Sarah, how are you? I am so sorry about your brother, I

know how much you thought of him," Edward said sympathetically.

The tears welled up in Sarah's eyes again and with a heavy heart, she said, "Thank you, Edward, for your kind words, me and my family do appreciate it, even though they have not met you yet."

"As a matter of fact, I was talking about you with my father earlier," Sarah added.

"All good I hope, Sarah!" Edward said nervously.

"Now that would be telling, wouldn't it? Sarah said, laughing.

It wouldn't do any harm to keep him guessing, as it was all in fun. They often teased one another about different things, having a similar sense of humour. Edward was never completely sure how to take Sarah half of the time, but even so, he still would have been willing to make her his wife, if she would only consent to be.

"Sarah, may I come and visit you tomorrow, if that's OK with you?" Edward asked.

"I will have to ask my parents, Edward. Just a moment," Sarah said.

"Mother and Father, Edward would like to come and see us tomorrow. His employers have given him some more time to say his goodbyes. He leaves on Wednesday now," Sarah said.

"Of course, dear, we will make a special tea for your friend," Mother said.

"There is no need to go to any bother, Mum, we will just have one of your special pies," Sarah said smiling.

Edward sounded pleased, and arranged with Sarah to meet at the train station as he had never been to that area before and did not want to get lost.

Just then Gregory came charging through the back door, like a bull in a china shop, as Father always said. He had been to see his boss at the bakery; he had given Gregory two boxes of cream cakes.

People were being so kind and couldn't seem to do enough for them at this time of great sadness in their lives. Gregory too was in the fortunate position of having a good boss. Sarah looked at him; heartache was written all over his face; her young brother was suffering too, but at seventeen was trying so hard to be strong, and in her heart she felt for him so much. He had really looked up to Edmund, and they too had been very close.

"How long will you be home for, Sare?" Gregory asked. He had called her by this special name since he was little.

"I don't know yet, Greg, I will have to see," Sarah replied.

"Sarah is having a gentleman visitor tomorrow by the name of Edward," Father said grinning.

"Oh yes? You are a dark horse! What's he like then?" Gregory asked inquisitively.

"You will have to wait and see like everyone else, won't you?" Sarah said.

"Are you OK now, Mother?" Gregory asked.

"Not too bad now, son," Mother said.

Sarah stared at her mother across the table; she didn't think that she would be able to look at her in the same way again. Sarah felt deeply let down and saddened by this thought.

Alice came in and went straight to Sarah; although Alice was in actual fact the youngest in the family, she had an old head on young shoulders, as some would say. She was only sixteen.

"Sarah, would you like to come along to choir practice with me tonight? I wasn't going to go, but I know that really Edmund would still want me to. He loved music so much," Alice said tearfully.

"Seeing as you put it like that, Alice, maybe we should try and go for Edmund's sake. If it's too much for us we can always come home. The minister will understand, won't he Alice?" Sarah said.

"I am sure he will. Now, let's try and eat our meal, we need to keep our strength up," Alice replied.

Dinner was soon over with as no one had much of an appetite; there was an uneasy silence in the room. They were all beginning to face the harsh reality that life would never be quite the same again for their family, without Edmund's warmth and his vivacious personality around.

Sarah and Alice made a start on the dishes; Sarah felt a sense of relief to get out of the room as she was beginning to feel the strain of it all again.

"What is all this about you and a gentleman, Sarah?" Alice asked.

"Oh, nothing much, he's just a friend. He is coming tomorrow to see me as he has to go overseas in a few days," Sarah said.

"Is he in the services then?" Alice enquired.

"No, he is a valet, and that is the end of the interrogation for now!" Sarah said sharply.

"I'm sorry," said Alice.

They soon finished clearing everything up and went upstairs to get ready to go out. After they had said their goodbyes, and Father said they had to be back for ten o'clock, they made their way down the road. Alice suddenly turned to Sarah and said, "Would you mind if we didn't actually go to choir practice tonight?"

"Why not? I thought you enjoyed going there, Alice?" Sarah asked. She was rather surprised at this request.

"Well, I did, but then for the past couple of weeks I haven't been going because I have been meeting someone," Alice said defensively.

"I don't believe I am hearing this! I have just about had enough lies in this family!" Sarah snapped angrily.

Alice was completely stunned by this remark, to say the

least. She could not understand why Sarah would say such a thing.

"What on earth do you mean by that?" Alice said.

"Nothing at all, forget I said anything," shouted Sarah.

"Well, it doesn't sound like nothing, Sarah, you sounded pretty angry to me!" Alice said.

"It doesn't matter, honestly. Can we change the subject please?" Sarah pleaded. "What I really want to know is who have you been meeting for the past two weeks? Do I know this person at all?" Sarah asked, with a certain amount of curiosity.

"No, actually it's a lad at work. He's called Jimmy Thompson, we have been seeing each other but the snag is Father doesn't approve of him at all," Alice said desperately. "His father, Harold, and him are both very active in the union, and Father calls them troublemakers," Alice added.

"You obviously don't agree with him, Alice, I can see that. So is that where you want to go now, to meet this boy?" Sarah asked.

"Please don't tell Father; he truly doesn't understand and just won't listen to me, and besides which, it's not fair to upset him at the moment, after losing our Edmund!" Alice pleaded with Sarah.

"I won't say anything for now, Alice, but you are going to have to discuss it with Father at some point, as deceit doesn't do anyone any good, believe me," Sarah said bluntly.

"Thanks Sarah, I will try to talk to him in a while, I promise," Alice replied.

As they went further down the road, a flat-capped figure emerged from under the lamplight and came towards them.

"Hello Alice, how are you? I am so sorry about your Edmund, and this must be big sister Sarah. I have heard so much about you," Jimmy said.

"Well, I, unlike you, have only just heard about your existence walking up the road with my little sister," Sarah said with a very straight face; it took her all her energy not to burst out laughing.

"That sounds a bit ominous," Jimmy said nervously.

"Take no notice of her, let's go and have a coffee in our usual café," Alice said.

Sarah thought to herself that this boy had a certain charm and a way about him; she could see why Alice liked him. They reached the café and managed to find a quiet corner, and ordered coffee. Alice looked at Sarah anxiously and said to her, "We need to talk to you, Sarah. Jimmy and I need your help."

Sarah began to get worried; she wondered what on earth they were going to say to her. Her imagination began to run riot.

"Sarah, Jimmy and I have been seeing each other for quite a while now, and we love one another and the thing is that I am not sure, but I think I am going to have a baby!"

Was this really Alice was saying these things? Sensible Alice who was always so responsible and practical? Sarah felt completely stunned. Alice only sixteen years of age! Father would probably lynch both of them and her as well!

What a day it had been for her. She had buried her brother and found out about her mother and Lord Chandler, then this.

"Please say something, Sarah, even if it is only to say how stupid you think we are," Alice said.

"I think you had better find out whether you are going to have a baby or not. If you are scared I will go with you to the doctor and it will all be confidential so Mother and Father needn't know for now," Sarah said.

"How can you? You will have to go back to work soon won't you Sarah?" Alice replied.

"No, I am never going back to that job," Sarah snapped. "And further more, I don't wish to talk about it at the moment, OK?"

"All right, calm down, Sarah. I didn't realise that it was a sensitive subject," Alice said.

"Well, let's just concentrate on you two for now and think how we are going to handle this situation," Sarah said.

She thought she sounded so calm, but the truth was Sarah was really worried, particularly about what her father would do about the situation if he found out.

"Alice, I need to ask you something, and I don't mean any offence to you Jimmy, but it needs to be said: you are not doing all of this just to prove a point to Father, because he doesn't like Jimmy or his father, are you?" Sarah said.

"How could you say such a horrid thing, Sarah?" Alice said tearfully.

"I didn't mean to be horrible, it's just that this isn't like you at all," Sarah replied.

"I'm really sorry Sarah, but Jimmy and I have true feelings for each other and we've asked you along tonight to let you know because I value your opinion," Alice said helplessly.

"Believe me, you wouldn't want to know my honest opinion at the moment," Sarah said sharply.

"That's just it; we really do," Jimmy said. Up to that moment he had said nothing, just sat looking at Alice and Sarah.

"Sarah, I do love your sister, and I will take care of her, no matter what happens," Jimmy explained.

Sarah was certainly no expert on relationships, but yet there seemed to be a certain kind of sincerity in his voice. They were so young. Alice was sixteen and Jimmy only eighteen; what could they possibly know about life? Sarah looked at her watch. It was nine thirty; they must go now in order not to be late home.

"Alice, we will have to be setting off now. It was nice to meet you, Jimmy, I hope everything works out for you two if that's what you want," Sarah said with concern in her voice.

"Thank you for coming, Sarah, and for listening to us. I know it meant a lot to Alice," Jimmy replied.

"That was the easy part. The hardest part will be convincing Mother and Father about your relationship," Sarah said.

Jimmy said he would walk them up to where he had met them and when they reached there he bid them both goodnight and said to Alice he would see her in a couple of days when she returned to work.

When he was out of sight, Alice said, "So tell me really what do you think of him honestly?"

"He seems OK, but I can't help worrying, you are both so young to be so serious," Sarah said anxiously.

"I just know, Sarah, that he is the one for me as you will know when you meet the right gentleman," Alice said defensively.

"Come on, let's get home. We've done enough gabbing for one night. Tomorrow I have to meet my friend Edward," Sarah said.

They rushed up the street. They could see a tall figure on their doorstep and they knew it would be Father looking for them.

"You are just on time, another few minutes and you would have been in real trouble. I am already very angry as you have lied to me about where you were going!" Father said sharply.

How on earth had he found out that they weren't going to choir practice? They were for it now!

"Inside you girls, I think you owe us some sort of explanation, don't you?" Mother said, looking at them both. "Could you tell me and your father exactly where you two have been then?"

"Half of this family seem to be lying about a lot of things lately," Sarah snapped, glaring at her mother.

"Since your brother died, Sarah, you seem to have been

very rude at times, my girl! I know that you're upset – we all are – but its no way to carry on," her father said.

"Its more than that, Father; why don't you ask Mother about it? She knows what I mean," Sarah said.

Sarah's mother's face drained of colour and she couldn't believe that Sarah was going to make her tell Harry about this, after all these years of it being a secret, known only to her, Vernon and now unfortunately by chance to Sarah.

"Well, what is that supposed to mean? Is anyone going to tell me, because none of us are going to bed until this is sorted out once and for all!" Father said angrily.

"I'm so sorry, Harry, I've wanted to tell you for a long time, but never been able to find the right words, or the right time," Mother replied, sobbing.

"Whatever do you mean by that, Mother? You are beginning to worry me now. All these years we have never had any secrets from each other. We have always been honest with one another, haven't we?" Father said, looking for some kind of reassurance.

"I hope you can forgive me for this… I am so sorry; many years ago, just before I met you, Harry, there was a man called Vernon Chandler. He was a fine man and we were very much in love, but his parents were very wealthy, and as I came from a poor, working-class family they forbade us to marry and stopped us from seeing one another by sending Vernon off abroad. At first I was absolutely heartbroken. We tried to write but our letters were intercepted by his family and probably destroyed, or so his mother took great delight in telling me," Sarah's mother said.

"So why have you never told me? That is not so bad, love," Father replied nervously.

"Because I am afraid that wasn't all. Our son Edmund was Vernon's baby. I am so sorry Harry!" Sarah's mother broke down again at this point and sobbed uncontrollably at the table.

"I can't believe this. How could you do this to me after everything we've been through together? Did Edmund know about this?" Father shouted.

"No, he knew nothing; as far as he was concerned you were his father, and you know he loved you very much!"

"God, I feel so mad that you have lied to me like this. I don't know if I can forgive you for this!" Father cried.

He was so angry, Sarah had never seen him in such a rage and she wasn't surprised either. In one way Sarah felt relieved that it was out in the open, and in another way she felt guilty that she had caused such an argument between her mother and father. Now everything would be different! Sarah just knew they would lose the closeness that they had always maintained through times of hardship.

So what now? She hoped they wouldn't decide to separate, but the question was, could they ever survive such a thing coming out into the open? This was certainly going to test the strength of their feelings, to the limit! Sarah's father slumped onto the sofa, his face was screwed up in pain and he looked as though he was struggling to get his breath. By this time Sarah's mother had left the room and gone upstairs crying.

"Father, what's wrong? Are you all right?" Sarah asked with concern.

"I've got a pain in my chest, it's all right don't fuss! I've had it before a few days ago, I'll be OK!" Father said.

"You don't look all right! I'm going next door to Mrs Williams to see if she could take us to the hospital. Alice, get Father a glass of water. I'll be as quick as I can," Sarah shouted.

Alice went to the kitchen. She was still reeling from what had been said. She could hardly believe it! It was definitely not the time to tell her parents about her relationship with Jimmy. She would have to let things quieten down a bit first, if they ever did. And as for the business about the baby, it would probably be best if she definitely had it confirmed by the doctor before she broke the news to her parents.

Alice gave her father the glass of water. She didn't like the colour he had gone at all, but him getting so angry wouldn't have helped matters.

Father took a small sip of water and said quietly, "So where were you and Sarah, Alice? You didn't tell us, did you?"

"There'll be plenty of time for that when you are feeling better, Father," Alice replied.

"What's wrong, Harry? And where's Sarah gone?" Mother asked as she walked into the room.

"What do you care about me? Maybe it might be better if I died too then you could go back to your precious Vernon fella!"

"Oh, how could you be so horrible? You don't know what it was like. It was a very difficult situation for us, but I do love you and I have made a different life for myself with you, Harry Watkins, and yes I care very much about you, you old fool, and I always will!"

"You got that right! I have been a fool, haven't I?" Father said helplessly.

"This isn't helping at all," Alice shouted.

Just then Sarah came back with Mrs Williams from next door. For most of the journey to the hospital Sarah's father kept insisting he was OK, but his face told a different story. When they got inside the hospital. Father was taken away by a nurse to be examined by one of the doctors and they were told not to worry. That was easier said than done!

The three of them sat in the waiting room feeling terribly guilty, all for their own reasons, and hardly speaking to one another. There was a large clock ticking loudly on the wall, and outside they could hear the clatter of trolleys up and down the corridor. It was midnight and still they sat waiting for someone to come and tell them how Father was. Sarah said she would take a walk down the corridor and try and find someone.

A very distinguished looking man came towards her. "Are you a relation of Mr Watkins?"

"Yes, I am one of his daughters, doctor. Please could you tell us how he is?" Sarah asked.

"You can see him now. Is anyone else here with you? He mentioned his wife."

"She is here waiting, doctor," Sarah said.

"Your father has had a slight heart attack. We will have to keep him in for a few days to do some tests on him."

"Thank you, doctor, so much," Sarah replied, feeling a little relieved but still concerned about the situation.

Sarah couldn't help feeling it was all her fault; she wondered if she hadn't said anything, would her father have been all right? It was too late now to reproach herself.

When Sarah got back to the waiting room there was only Alice there. Mother had apparently gone out for some air. Sarah told Alice that Father was OK but that he would have to stay in hospital for a few days.

"Oh my goodness, he will hate that. You know how he dislikes any kind of fuss," Mother said as she came back through the door. "Sarah, did they say what is wrong with your father?"

"He has had a mild heart attack so he has to take it easy for a while and they will have to carry out some tests on him," Sarah said.

They all made their way up the corridor and could hear Father telling a nurse he would be going home that evening.

"It's just a bit of indigestion. I'll be OK after a good night's kip in my own bed at home," he insisted.

"I am afraid that won't be possible, Mr Watkins, you have had a mild heart attack and we will have to run a series of tests on you," the nurse said sharply.

"Tests? What kind of tests? I have never had a day's illness in my life!" Father said with astonishment. "It is about time you three came in here! Where have you been?" he said.

"Waiting to see you, Father!" Alice replied reassuringly.

"You are in the best place, Pop, they will look after you. Maybe you have been overdoing things without realising it," Sarah added.

"Sarah, shall we go and see if we can get a cup of tea or something?" Alice asked, hoping that they could leave their parents alone for a while to air their differences.

"Oh right, OK, see you in a minute," Sarah said.

When they had gone Mother said, "Harry, are you OK? I am so sorry about everything. I don't want to lose you, I love you and always have. You are a good man, I know that much."

"And I love you. Do you think we will ever be able to put this behind us and start again? Edmund wouldn't have wanted the pair of us at each other's throats. I was really scared, love, when I got those pains in my chest. I thought I was going to die! They were worse than the last time,"

"How could you not tell me about this?" Mother snapped.

"It happened at work in the changing rooms but the pain soon went off again… Promise me, love, no more secrets no matter what happens – I mean it!"

"I promise, Harry. It was a stupid mistake and I should have known better."

The girls returned with cups of tea and smiled at one another. They could see that things were a little better as Mother was holding Father's hand.

"You needn't worry, girls, there is not going to be any more yelling. Apart from the fact that it's not good for my old ticker, we are going to try and sort things out for Edmund's sake," Father said.

"But you two still owe us an explanation of your whereabouts last night, but that can wait till the morning. Now we have to go home and let your father get some sleep," Mother said. "I will be back in the morning, Harry, with some clean pyjamas and some of your wireless magazines; is there anything else you want, love?"

"Yes, a packet of those nice fig roll biscuits, if this lot will let me have them," Father added.

"I will see you, love. Bye for now," Mother replied.

As they walked out of the hospital, Mother said, "I don't want Brenda and Gregory to know anything about me and your dad's argument tonight, there is no need for them to find out. There has been enough upset," Mother pleaded.

So they promised not to mention anything. Sarah didn't want to be unkind, but couldn't help thinking that if it had been Brenda asked to keep something quiet, she would have found it virtually impossible! Brenda couldn't help it; she never could keep a secret. In other respects she was a good sister and always full of fun, but just not very discreet.

When they got home Brenda and Gregory were sat having a cup of tea before they both had to go to work. The others had scribbled down a note for them to explain about going to the hospital.

"What was all the shouting about last night when I was out? Mrs Williams' daughter Celia said there was a right racket going on," Gregory said.

"Oh, it was just your father throwing his weight about because Sarah and Alice were late home," Mother said.

"Where did you two get to then? We know you didn't go to choir practice because the vicar phoned up," Brenda said smugly.

"We had to go and see one of my friends who has a bit of a problem, it's personal, and then we called for some chips on the way home," Sarah said defensively. She couldn't believe how quickly she had come up with an instant excuse. Brenda didn't pursue the matter any further. She was more interested for the moment in how Father was.

"Is Father going to be OK then?" Brenda asked with concern.

"I think so, love. He will have to stay in hospital for a few days' rest, and he has to have some tests done on his heart," Mother said, trying her best to reassure them that everything would be all right.

"We can go and see him though, can't we?" Gregory asked.

"Of course. You can go tomorrow after work if you want to," Mother replied.

"We need to get some sleep. Sarah, aren't you supposed to be meeting your friend at the station this morning?" Mother enquired.

"Oh no! I had forgotten all about that with Father being taken ill," Sarah said. "I wonder if I could phone him and see him tomorrow instead?" she added.

"He will have set off by now, won't he?" Alice replied.

"I will just have to pinch an hour's sleep on the sofa then, I suppose," Sarah said wearily.

Brenda and Gregory went to work and the others tried to get some rest. Sarah was woken up suddenly by the phone ringing. She got up still feeling tired; it was Edward at the station.

"I thought you were coming to meet me, are you still able to, Sarah?" Edward asked.

"Yes, but I will be there in about half an hour, I'm sorry. Can you get a coffee? I will explain when I see you," Sarah said briefly.

"OK, see you in a while Sarah," Edward said.

Sarah would explain about her father's heart attack when she saw him. And she would not be mentioning her parents' row, even though she didn't approve of the situation there was still such a thing as family loyalty.

Sarah arrived at the station and after searching for a

while she found Edward in one of the restaurants staring into his coffee cup.

"Penny for them, then?" Sarah asked him.

"They are worth a lot more than that, Sarah – well, as far as I am concerned anyway," Edward said seriously.

"This is a heavy conversation for this time of the morning, especially as I hardly had any sleep last night," Sarah said.

"Why? What's wrong Sarah? What I have to say to you will wait; I have waited this long," Edward replied.

"To be honest, Edward, I didn't think you would speak to me again after the way I treated you last time we met," Sarah said cautiously.

"Sarah, I care for you an awful lot. I always want us to be friends, more than that really, as you already know," Edward added, his voice filled with emotion.

"I know, and I am sorry but last night we had to take my father to hospital," Sarah continued.

"My goodness, is he all right Sarah?"

"I think he is going to be OK. He has had a mild heart attack, so he has to stay in hospital for a few days so they can do some tests," Sarah replied.

"Well, I'm sure they will take good care of him," Edward said, trying to sound reassuring.

"I know, but he scared the life out of us last night and we were up at the hospital most of the night," Sarah said with concern in her voice.

"I would have said to meet you another day but I haven't much time left, Sarah. You know that I have to leave for Switzerland in two days' time," Edward urged.

"I thought we had been over all this before, Edward? I can't possibly go with you," Sarah repeated.

"Sarah, I am begging you to reconsider. I want to spend the rest of my life with you. I know that you have said that you don't love me but you are fond of me, aren't you? And fondness could grow into love," Edward said desperately.

Sarah looked hard at Edward and saw before her a fine honest man who truly seemed to care for her. Maybe she should think again? After all, what had Yorkshire or London to offer her now? If she did go with Edward it could be on her terms, and he was a good man and a true friend to her, which was especially what she needed; now more than ever.

"Edward, if I was to change my mind could we take things very slowly, maybe with a view to marriage in the near future? I'm not ruling out the possibility altogether," she said.

"Sarah, you won't regret this, believe me! I will make you a very happy woman, I promise," Edward said excitedly. "But, what about your position at Swarbrick Manor? Will you have to give any notice?"

"No, don't worry, everything will be OK. I will talk to Lord Chandler tonight," Sarah said sharply.

"You will love Switzerland, I just know it, Sarah. It is a whole different way of life over there. The air is so fresh and crisp," Edward said, with such enthusiasm and longing in his voice.

"How do you know such things, Edward, anyway?" she asked.

"Because I have been there for a visit. I didn't get round to telling you because you dashed off when I saw you, didn't you?" Edward said sadly.

"I'm sorry, Edward, I have been awful to you lately, but I will make it up to you, honest I will," she said determinedly.

"All I ask of you is that you come with me and we will have a brand new life together," Edward said, smiling at her.

"Well, what shall we do now? I suppose we could go back to my house and have some lunch? I'm sorry that you won't be able to meet my father, but maybe another time," Sarah announced.

"At least I will meet your mother. You have told me so much about her, Sarah," he said.

"I was thinking, I know that it is a lot to ask, but could we keep this between the two of us just for now, till I find a way to tell my parents? Believe me, they wouldn't thank me for springing something like this upon them at the moment," Sarah said.

"I think I understand, just as long as you don't change your mind, Sarah. You won't, will you?" Edward asked desperately.

"No, honestly; now I am set upon the idea, I won't, I promise," she said. "Also, could we have a bit more time – say till Friday – for them to get used to the idea? As it is going to be a bit of a shock for them, taking the news in, and then me flying off to another country, couldn't you explain to your employer about my father being taken ill?" Sarah asked.

"I will try my best. My employer is fairly reasonable. I will call you tomorrow if that's OK," Edward replied.

"That's fine. Let's go and catch the bus home, and I will make you one of my special cups of tea," Sarah laughed.

"Sounds good to me," Edward said, taking Sarah's arm.

They walked out of the station. Sarah was definitely warming to the idea of changing her life. The family would be very surprised, but hopefully when they had got over the shock they would be very happy for her and Edward. And possibly they would grow to be as fond of Edward as she was.

In the meantime, the sun was shining brightly and Edward felt ten feet tall as he strolled along with the woman he loved, and he couldn't wait to begin their new life. He knew he could make Sarah happy given the chance to prove it.

As they walked in the back door voices were raised.

"I'm sorry about this, Edward, it's not usually like this!" Sarah said, trying to hide her embarrassment.

"Don't worry, Sarah, everyone has disagreements sometimes," Edward assured her.

Alice stormed passed them shouting, "I am not a child anymore, I am a young woman, and it's my life. I can do what I want!"

"While you live here you will do as I say, my girl! If your father wasn't ill he would have something to say about this! I'm not going to worry him now. Going out with Jimmy Thompson indeed!" Mother shouted angrily. She suddenly noticed Sarah and Edward standing in the doorway.

"Oh, I am so sorry about that. Your sister has become so headstrong lately! It's not like her at all… Do come in and have a cup of tea." Mother led them into the parlour.

Edward took off his cap and jacket and sat down on the sofa. Mother had prepared some sandwiches, pie and cakes. Sarah felt quite pleased and couldn't help wondering what her mother would think of her plans when she found out…

"Edward, do you mind if I go and see if Alice is OK?" Sarah asked.

"No, of course not, Sarah, I will be all right," Edward replied.

"Don't forget; don't say anything to Mother about us," Sarah whispered as she passed Edward.

She found Alice outside near the lamppost where they had met Jimmy the previous night. "Why on earth did you tell Mother about Jimmy now? I thought you were going to wait a while," Sarah asked.

"I know, Mother just got me so angry! I have a life too, as well as everyone else, you know," Alice snapped.

"You didn't tell her about the baby as well, did you Alice?" Sarah asked warily.

"No, but I nearly did. If I hadn't walked out I think I would have done," Alice said sharply.

"I don't know, this family used to be so close and now it seems since our Edmund died that it's falling apart," Sarah said with a deep sadness in her voice.

Sarah knew that the dreadful news of Edmund's death

had knocked them all for six, but finding out about the other business seemed just as much of a shock! Also, although her news was going to be good news, it would still be another kind of shock for them all. Sarah needed to sit them down quietly and tell them all, except for Father. Maybe Mother would do that for her. After tea tonight would be as good a time as any.

"Won't you come back home with me, Alice? You'll feel better when you have had one of my cups of tea," Sarah smiled, trying to cheer her sister up.

"OK then, as long as Mother doesn't say anything else to me tonight; I don't think I could bear it. To listen to her and Father you would think my Jimmy was some sort of monster," Alice added resentfully.

"Never mind, Alice, they will calm down eventually. I'm sure things will turn out all right in the end, you'll see," Sarah said reassuringly. They walked back into the kitchen. The wireless was on and Edward and Mother were chatting quite happily together.

"Are you girls going to have a sandwich then?" Mother asked.

Mother looked at them both together, as thick as thieves, and she thought how much Sarah reminded her of herself when she was young.

They sat around talking and Gregory and Brenda came in from work for their lunch and joined in the conversation. It had been quite a pleasant afternoon and then at three o'clock, Sarah and Edward had to leave for the station. Gregory said he would be able to finish early to go with Sarah to the station to keep her company on the way home.

Edward said goodbye to Sarah at the station and promised to call the next day with his employer's decision. As Sarah and Gregory walked to the bus, Gregory said, "What did Edward mean by what he said about his employer's decision?"

"You will find out in good time, Gregory. You needn't worry," Sarah said defensively.

Gregory wondered what it was all about, but there was one thing he had noticed and that was Sarah seemed different and quite happy for some reason. Could it be something to do with this gentleman they had met? No doubt they would find out in due course.

When they returned home Mother and Alice were in the kitchen preparing some tea.

"You two had better sit down. We have something to tell you both," Mother said with a note of concern in her voice.

"Don't tell me it's Father, I couldn't stand it! Is he all right?" Sarah pleaded.

"No, love, don't worry, Father is OK. It's something else I have to tell you. We had a phone call after you left for the station."

"Who was it from, Mother?" Gregory enquired.

"Just a moment, son, and I will tell you both. It was from a young lady who called herself Sally Whittaker. She was a friend of our Edmund's and worked with him."

"Oh," said Sarah anxiously, as she knew of this lady but had been sworn to secrecy by Edmund; obviously he was fond of her. Sarah was finding it a little awkward trying to pretend that she didn't know of Sally, but somehow she managed to convince everyone anyway.

"Well, that's not all. It appears they had got engaged to be married and were going to come and see us on their next leave."

"Oh, what news! It's such a pity that things have turned out like this," Brenda sobbed. It was the first time she had cried since Edmund had died.

Mother tried to comfort her as best she could. "And Sally is expecting our Edmund's baby. She would like to come and see us and didn't want to just spring the news on us when she came," Mother said with a mixture of emotions.

"Oh my goodness, Mother, I can't believe it," Sarah said, with tears welling up in her eyes.

"Sally wants to call tomorrow at about eleven in the morning. I feel so nervous and kind of excited," Mother replied.

Sarah thought that there would be two kinds of exciting news: what she had just heard and her own news! Both were going to change things in the family for ever, but at least Sarah would be able to visit her family when she went away. She would be going on an aeroplane for the first time in her life – how exciting it was going to be, never mind becoming an auntie to her brother's child, a brother who she had adored so much.

"I can't get over how something so special could come out of such a tragedy like Edmund's death," Mother said emotionally.

"It will be like having a small part of Edmund still with us, won't it? Especially if it is a boy," Brenda said, smiling a little.

They got their meal underway in silence and enjoyed one of Mother's home-made pies. Sarah looked across at her mother. "I have some news of my own to tell you all. You know my gentleman friend, Edward, that you met? Well, we have been seeing one another for quite some time and have grown very fond of each other. And well, Edward has asked me to get engaged and to join him working in Switzerland. We will possibly be leaving on Friday," Sarah said excitedly.

"Oh my goodness gracious, Sarah! I can't believe it, I don't know what your father is going to make of all this!" Mother exclaimed. It was all too much to take in at once. The doctors at the hospital had said that Father wasn't to have any sudden shocks or undue stress! How on earth was she going to break all of this news to him? The moment would have to be chosen very carefully. And as for Sarah, she would have to have a quiet word with her father at some point. She couldn't exactly just go off to Switzerland without a word; that would upset him so much; she owed her father far more than that.

Alice and Mother had managed to patch things up and Mother was going to try and persuade Father to let Alice see Jimmy; she had been young herself once, and Jimmy couldn't be all bad if he thought so much of her daughter. A few words of persuasion from Sarah had helped her see things from a different point of view.

After their meal Alice and Sarah cleared the dishes and Alice whispered to Sarah, "You know you said you would come with me to the doctor's? Well, I have got an appointment for tomorrow morning. Will you come with me?" Alice pleaded.

"Of course I will, then afterwards I will have to take the train and go to see my employers and pick up my belongings," Sarah said coldly. "How have you managed to get the time off work, Alice?"

"I said I had an appointment at the dentist, so it's OK," Alice replied nervously.

"You'll be all right, sis, don't worry," Sarah said calmly. "Mother, can I make a brief phone call? I need to call up Swarbrick Manor about collecting my things," Sarah asked.

"Yes of course, dear. I hope you are able to sort things out," Mother said apprehensively.

Sarah sat and began to make her call. The phone rang several times before anyone answered. Suddenly it was Blake's voice on the line. "Sarah, is that you? How are things with your family now? Everyone here sends their condolences."

"Thank you so much. I wonder if I could speak to Lord Chandler?" Sarah enquired.

"Just one moment, I will tell him you wish to speak to him," Blake replied. Then there were a few moments of

The Winds of Change

silence, which seemed to last a while to Sarah, as she just wanted to get the whole business over and done with.

"Sarah, how are you dear? Are you going to come back to us presently?" Lord Chandler asked nervously.

Sarah couldn't believe the nerve of the man! Talking to her like that as though nothing had happened! Well, she for one would not forget what had occurred, and she would keep her conversation polite but to the point.

"I don't think that would be a good idea at all. I would like to come and collect my belongings tomorrow, as I have the opportunity of another position abroad," Sarah said coldly.

Lord Chandler hesitated then he said, "Oh, I see. Then we won't expect you back, under the circumstances. We will see you tomorrow, is eleven o'clock OK? Goodbye then, Sarah, take care," Lord Chandler replied, his voice quivering with emotion.

Sarah felt a little sorry for him in a way, as he had lost a son; but he could never have loved Edmund as much as her, as he was a very special part of her family and their lives would never be the same without him.

Sarah said goodbye and sat thinking of how different her life was going to be. As she came around to the idea more she had a good kind of feeling about it all. Then she thought of Alice – poor Alice, she was a mere young girl. Maybe it would be for the best if she was not pregnant. Sarah wasn't being unkind, it was just that it was such a big responsibility bringing up a baby. She herself wasn't ready for such things, let alone her younger sister.

But she knew that no matter what happened, when things had calmed down if Alice was pregnant she would receive plenty of support; that's what their family was about.

"Was everything all right with your phone call Sarah? It's just that you look so worried," Mother said, somewhat concerned.

"No, it was fine Mother. I have to go at eleven tomorrow, and I will bring my belongings back. Hopefully I shall be home for tea. Could you please make a meal for me anyway?" Sarah asked.

"Of course I will. I will make a nice hot pot, how about that? I'm sure you will be OK, Sarah love," Mother replied reassuringly.

Sarah just wanted to go and get back home and start planning the rest of her life.

The phone rang; it was Edward calling to say that his employers had said they could fly to Switzerland on Saturday and had made all the necessary arrangements. Edward's boss would meet them both at London airport on Saturday morning with the aeroplane tickets. Sarah began to feel quite excited by the prospect of it all and had arranged to see Edward on Friday, and Mother said he could stay overnight and sleep in Gregory's room so they could go to the airport together on Saturday.

She had so much to sort out in only a couple of days. Sarah went upstairs and began to try and sort out her clothes.

The next morning Sarah was up early, as she had promised Alice to go with her to her doctor's appointment. She felt so tired; she had hardly slept a wink, everything was going round in her head but she hoped that everything would turn out all right in the end, not just for her, but for all of the family. Time could be a healer, so people said. Sarah hoped it would help all of them.

Alice, on the other hand, was still sound asleep. Sarah woke her up with a cup of tea. "Come on, let's go and get this sorted out, shall we?" Sarah said.

"What are you two going to sort out at this time of the morning, I wonder?" Mother asked them. She hadn't been able to sleep and had got up to have a cup of tea. She would be going up to the hospital later to bring Father home. It was going to be difficult trying to get Father to take it easy and not to go ranting and raving about anything, like he normally did.

"Well, is anyone going to answer me then?" Mother asked again sharply.

"Oh, it's just Alice, Mother. She needs to see the dentist, and the big baby needs her big sister to go with her," Sarah said quickly.

"I see, well good luck – rather her than me! You know what I am like for the dentist," Mother replied.

"We had better get going soon, Sarah, we don't want to miss the bus," Alice said.

"See you two girls later," Mother said, and she took her cup of tea back upstairs.

Sarah and Alice rushed down the street and just caught their bus as it was pulling away from the stop. "We nearly missed it, sis, and what was that all about me being a big baby? Big baby indeed!" Alice replied laughing. If she was worried about things she certainly wasn't showing it.

Sarah waited as her sister went into the doctor's room. Her stomach was churning – she was feeling nervous enough for the both of them! Alice seemed to be in there for ages, and when she came out she was as white as a sheet. She walked over to Sarah.

"Can we just go now? I need some fresh air," Alice said.

"You certainly look like you need some, Alice! Are you going to tell me what's wrong before I have to go and get my train to pick up my things from the Manor?" Sarah asked with a note of concern in her voice.

"Well, I will say this much Sarah; lately certain people in this family don't seem to be doing things by halves; there is you flying off to Switzerland at the end of the week to make a new life for yourself and there's me and Jimmy going to have twins," Alice replied, sounding partly excited and scared as well.

"*What?*" Sarah shouted.

"Yes, you heard me right, so now what do I do?" Alice said, beginning to cry.

"Don't upset yourself, Alice, it'll be all right, you'll see, and it's not good for the babies when you get worked up – so the experts say," Sarah added, only trying to be helpful.

"Damn the experts! How on earth am I going to tell Mother and Father about this?" Alice cried.

"We will find a way, and I will be there for you when you tell them. It will be a shock for them – there's no denying that – but I am sure that they will help you any way they can when they have got over it," Sarah added, trying to sound convincing to reassure her sister.

Sarah always thought that she would be the first one to start a family, so this all seemed a bit strange to her. Her little sister was going to be a mother! Sarah hoped that her parents would be OK about things and that this boy Jimmy was going to take good care of her baby sister. Time would tell whether his feelings were sincere or not, she supposed.

"Let's go and get a bite to eat in that café we went in the other night, then I will have to go and catch my train. Will you be all right, Alice? I will see you later and we will talk to Mother tonight and find a way to break the news to Father," Sarah said calmly.

"I couldn't eat anything, my stomach's doing cartwheels at the moment, I just feel sick!" Alice said nervously.

"Well, just have a glass of milk then," Sarah suggested.

So they both sat only half listening to each other, trying to take the news in. "Edmund would have made a brilliant uncle, he loved kids," Sarah said regretfully.

"And we are going to be aunties to his child in the near future, such a great shame he didn't live to be a dad," Alice said with deep regret. "They say only the good die young, and he certainly was one of the best, wasn't he?"

"I know, but there's one thing he wouldn't want us to do and that would be to sit here all morbid, so let's think about the future and those two lovely babies that you are going to bring into the world," Sarah said thoughtfully.

"Gosh, when you put it like that, Sarah, it sounds such a big responsibility doesn't it?" Alice said nervously.

"That's because it is; that will be our next generation. You know, I envy you in a way, having a family. Children can bring so much love and it's unconditional and they need you to care for them completely," Sarah said.

"Sarah Watkins, is that really you saying such things? I never thought that I would see the day! I thought that you were the career woman of the family," Alice said smiling.

"I know, but so much has happened lately and when we lost our Edmund it really made me think; life is too short. We should all just make the best of our lives. After all, you only get one, don't you sis?" Sarah replied.

"Well, that's true enough. I don't feel too bad now, Sarah, so I'll see you to the station and go back to work. Heaven only knows how I am going to get any work done, I won't be able to concentrate on anything!" Alice said.

They caught the bus to the station and sat for some reason reminiscing about when they were children, and laughed so much together that they nearly missed their stop. When they got off, the heavens seemed to open and they both made a dash for shelter inside the station.

"Try not to worry. I'll be home later. If you want to get the bus now, Alice, I will be fine," Sarah said.

"I think I will get out of this rain. Good luck at the Manor, hope everything goes OK for you," Alice added, and she disappeared round the corner.

Ten minutes later Sarah's train came, she sat glancing through a magazine she had purchased at the station the idea being to take her mind off things a bit. But it didn't really help at all; as the stations passed by the window her mind was full of all the things that had happened lately. As Sarah approached her station she couldn't help wondering whether Lady Chandler had any knowledge of the situation between her mother and Lord Chandler. Sarah pitied her really, as she had a very likeable disposition and had always been kindness itself to Sarah.

As Sarah got off the train Blake appeared smiling.

"I didn't really expect anyone to meet me," Sarah said.

"Lord Chandler instructed me to do so, Sarah," Blake added in his usual matter-of-fact manner.

"I bet he did," Sarah muttered under her breath.

"Did you say something, Sarah?" Blake enquired.

"Nothing," Sarah said quickly.

They drove back to the Manor in silence. Blake still didn't quite know what to say to Sarah and she was trying hard to collect her thoughts. When they arrived at the Manor everyone was in the servants' quarters waiting to greet Sarah, she felt quite overwhelmed by such a reception! All in all she had enjoyed her time at the Manor, and in some respects she was going to miss her colleagues. Even Veronica had bought her a leaving gift, along with the others. There was the most exquisite pearl necklace and earrings from most of the servants, and Veronica's present was French perfume!

The cook had put on the most marvellous spread of food Sarah had ever seen. She felt very important, and expressed her gratitude accordingly. The party went on for a couple of hours, and Lord and Lady Chandler made a brief appearance to thank her for her service to their household and said they were sorry to see her go.

Lord Chandler stood awkwardly in a corner and couldn't seem to look Sarah in the eye; he left most of the talking to his wife, although he did give her an envelope, which he said contained a reference for any future employer. Sarah thanked him then excused herself and went up to her room to pack up her things. As she was getting them into suitcases there was a gentle tap on her door.

"Come in!" Sarah shouted.

It was Jenny. She seemed to be a little upset. "I'm really going to miss you, Sarah. You were the only one that I could talk to apart from cook."

"You'll be all right and we can write to one another, and you never know; in the future we may see each other again if we keep in touch. Do you promise to, Jenny?"

"I will, honest Sarah, and I will tell you all the latest that's happening at the dance – you know, the one we went to. Didn't we have fun Sarah?"

"Which part did you enjoy the most? Meeting those other girls and the blokes there, or breaking your arm?" Sarah laughed. She was always teasing Jenny but she didn't mind, as she was just as bad!

"Blake's face was an absolute picture when we got him out of bed, wasn't it?" Jenny said.

"Oh yes, I don't think he liked us disturbing his beauty sleep did he? Never mind," Sarah said cheekily.

Suddenly there was the sound of someone coughing outside the door. It was Blake. "Sarah, are you nearly packed up then? I can give you a lift back to the station," Blake said sternly.

"I will be out in about ten minutes, if that's OK Blake?" Sarah asked nervously.

"OK, I will see you in the main hallway downstairs. Perhaps Jenny will be good enough to help you with your lighter luggage when you both have finished your chat," Blake replied abruptly.

"Do you think he heard us, Sarah?" Jenny asked.

"It doesn't really matter now, does it?" Sarah said.

Jenny gave Sarah an enormous hug and wished her well in her new life. Sarah would miss Jenny too in a way, but she would try and keep in touch anyway. It had been a very pleasant afternoon – much better than she had anticipated. Sarah hadn't really known what to expect when she arrived.

She felt a great sense of relief that there had been no unpleasant scenes.

When Sarah had said all her goodbyes to everyone and was on the train going home, she settled herself with some coffee out of a thermos that cook had prepared for her journey and opened the envelope that Lord Chandler had given to her.

Inside there was a reference, and it was without a doubt the best one she had ever had. Her new employer would be very pleased with it. But that wasn't all that was in the envelope! There were two other letters, one was addressed to her and the other one was to her mother. She put her letter on the table in front of her and stared at her mother's letter suspiciously. She couldn't help wondering what that one contained. Sarah couldn't possibly open it – that wouldn't be right. And if she destroyed it that would be wrong also, but that is what she wanted to do. She wished the whole ghastly business had never happened at all.

But then, what was she thinking, that she wished Edmund had never been born? Not at all! He had been the best brother anyone could ever wish for, so she supposed she would have to give her mother the letter no matter what she thought, simply because it was the right thing to do. Sarah just hoped it would not be the cause of any more sorrow and trouble. They had all had their share already, especially her poor father! Now was the time for all the family to look to the future, especially her and Alice. Sarah thought perhaps when she got back home she would have a quiet talk to Mother about Alice as she felt she should prepare her for such a shock. Even though they hadn't seen eye-to-eye lately, Sarah thought her mother didn't deserve to just have such a thing sprung upon her. Then afterwards Sarah would give her mother the letter.

When Sarah finally did get home, Father was having a lie

down upstairs and Mother was preparing the evening meal; toad in the hole with onion gravy, one of Sarah's favourites.

"Shall we have a cup of tea, love? Was everything all right at the Manor?" Mother asked with a note of concern.

"They put on a bit of a party for me, and bought me some presents, a beautiful pearl necklace with earrings and some French perfume," Sarah added.

"It sounds grand, I am pleased that you have had a nice time, and I still can't believe that my girl will be taking off to Switzerland on Saturday!" Mother said, her voice filled with emotion.

"Don't cry, Mother. Can we sit down? I need to talk to you about something else that is really important," Sarah said cautiously.

"Whatever is the matter, love? You know that you can tell me anything don't you?" Mother said trying to reassure Sarah, as she could see she was obviously anxious over something.

"Well, the thing is, Mother, it's not to do with me, it's about our Alice…" Sarah replied.

"What about Alice? Is there something wrong with her?" Mother asked nervously, she continued: "I honestly couldn't stand any more bad news at the moment!"

"Well, you know she has been seeing Jimmy Thompson, and they have grown quite fond of one another… well, the thing is she has been keeping something to herself for a few months… I am sorry, Mother, but she was scared what you and Father would say…" Sarah said defensively.

"She is pregnant, isn't she Sarah?"

"Yes, but she is going to have twins!"

"Oh my goodness! Fetch me a glass of sherry, Sarah, I can't believe this!" Mother said, shocked to have her suspicions confirmed. All of the colour drained from her face in exactly the same way that it had done with Alice when she had found out the news. Mother started to sob. Sarah put her arm around her to try to comfort her, and she sat hoping that Alice wouldn't be mad with her for telling her mother on her own.

"I am not angry you know, I realise she is very young but I feel somehow inside me that she would make a good mother."

"I know, but she will need a lot of support from all of us, won't she?" Sarah added with concern for her younger sister.

"After everything we have all been through lately, Sarah, it is wonderful to hear such happy news. Father will come round to the idea in time, I know he will," Mother said, still feeling shocked somewhat and yet a little excited too.

"You know I love you, don't you Mother? And Alice does too, we all do," Sarah said smiling.

"I know, Sarah love, and I love you too and I am so very proud of you. And so very sorry for all this trouble lately," her mother replied. They gave each other a hug and started to set the table for their meal. Afterwards they sat with a cup of tea on the sofa chatting.

"I have made some special cakes, and some extra ones for your special tea on Friday," Mother added.

"I am sure they will be lovely, but Mother, there is one more thing I need to tell you; when I came away from the Manor Lord Chandler handed me an envelope, which he said had a reference inside it. But there were also two other notes in it; one for you and one for me," Sarah said angrily.

"Oh!" Mother said anxiously as she looked at Sarah.

"So are you going to open it then or not?" Sarah asked.

"That is going where it belongs, straight into the bin!" Mother said sharply.

"And so can mine!" Sarah replied.

"I wish that I had never set eyes on that man," Mother said angrily.

"Never mind, Mother, at least one good thing came out of it – our Edmund!" Sarah said smiling.

The Winds of Change

"Of course, I wouldn't have swapped him or any of the rest of you for all the world," Mother replied proudly.

Just then Father called down: "Any chance of a cup of tea, after you two ladies have finished your chat down there?"

"OK, Harry love, I will bring you one up in a minute. I'll just check the oven – you don't want burnt offerings for your tea, do you now?" Mother shouted.

"Well, it will make our hair curl, won't it?" Father called out laughing.

"I will tell him something in a minute that will make his hair curl – I think I had better put a drop of brandy in that cup of tea for your father; somehow I think he is going to need it," Mother said to Sarah. Sarah looked up from her magazine and smiled at her mother; she was such a strong, determined woman who would do anything for her family and continued to cope with whatever came along in life. And that was just one of the things that Sarah loved about her.

"I'll be down in a bit, Sarah love. Will you keep an eye on the vegetables for me?" Mother asked.

"OK Mother, and I will make a fresh pot of tea since the others will be in from work soon," Sarah replied.

The meal was almost ready when Sarah's mother returned from upstairs. "Everything's going to be all right, I've had a quiet word with your father and all things considered he took the news rather well. Even managed to tell him about Edmund's girl as well."

"Gosh, what a lot for Father to find out about at once! What about my job in Switzerland? Did you tell him?" Sarah asked nervously.

"No, you go up now and talk to him. I thought you should tell him about that yourself. You do understand don't you Sarah?" Mother said.

"Yes, OK I will take him some more tea. I'll be down shortly," Sarah said.

Her father was sat up on the bed. Sarah went in and as she approached him he was wiping his eyes but he smiled when he saw her. "Are you OK, Pops? What did you think about the news then? It was quite something, wasn't it?" Sarah said.

"You can say that again, Sarah love, but raising the roof about it all won't do any of us any good, will it?" Father said quietly.

"That's true I suppose, and you know, Father, I'm sure everything will be all right in the end," Sarah added reassuringly.

Her father smiled at her. "Well blossom, I expect we will survive, won't we?"

"Father, I have some news of my own to tell you. I won't be going back to the Manor after all," Sarah said, looking for a reaction from her father.

"It's OK Sarah, I'm not annoyed. I was half expecting something like this, but what will you do for work instead, love?" Father said anxiously.

"Well, I have been offered another position with my gentleman friend Edward, the job is in Switzerland and he wishes us to get engaged!" Sarah replied excitedly.

"Just a minute, slow down! What did you say Sarah? You've got a job in Switzerland? And you're going to get engaged to be married?" Sarah's father stared at her with a complete look of disbelief. He couldn't believe it; his daughter engaged and off to another country!

"Well goodness me! I'm all right Sarah, don't look so worried, I'm really surprised that's all. I'll get used to things eventually, I'm sure. It just seems to have been a day for news, that's all," Father added.

"Do you want me to help you downstairs, Father?" Sarah asked.

"No, I'll be fine thank you, I'm not an invalid you know," Father said, laughing. Sarah smiled at him and walked behind him downstairs for tea.

Everyone was seated round the table, and they turned and looked at Father. "I wish everyone would stop fussing around me like mother hens. I'm all right, let's eat!" Father said.

Just as they were all finishing their meal, Father said, "After the sad time we have all had lately, it is nice to share some happy family news. You know that our Edmund's fiancée is coming to see us tomorrow; I hope we will all make her feel welcome. And it is such wonderful news about their baby," Father said, full of emotion.

"Also, our Alice is going to become a mother herself, and is going to have twins no less. Well, this family is certainly going to see some changes in the future, but no matter what we have got each other and we will help one another. That's what families are all about," Father said proudly.

"I love you, Father," Alice replied, with tears in her eyes.

"I know you do, and you don't need to worry about a thing; me and your mother will help you but we have discussed this, and sixteen is way too young to get wed. You can still see Jimmy as much as you like and he can help out with the babies when they arrive. And if you two still feel the same way when you are eighteen, then Mother and I will give you our blessing. And last but by no means least, our Sarah is going to get engaged and going off to Switzerland with her fiancé to a new job and new life. I always knew our Sarah would go far, but I didn't imagine it to be somewhere like Switzerland! Still, if that's what she wants, and as long as this Edward chap takes good care of her... otherwise him and I will be having some very serious words!"

Sarah's father smiled reassuringly across the table at Sarah and gave her a wink. She laughed and said, "Oh, Father, I am going to miss you and everyone else."

"You haven't gone yet, we've got a party to have, it's going to be the best ever! It will be a celebration we won't forget in a hurry," Father said with pride.

"Oh yes, Harry Watkins? You make it sound like the event of the year," Mother said.

"Nothing's too good for my kids, Mrs Watkins," Father said.

As they all got up from the table, Alice thanked Sarah for speaking to Mother on her behalf; she had definitely smoothed things over for her and Jimmy, and for that she would always be grateful to Sarah.

Sarah felt pleased that things had been sorted out before she went away; she was really going to miss all of her family but she knew they were all survivors like herself and they would all pull together.

Mother cleared everything away with Brenda helping her; Brenda asked her mother if she could speak to her.

"Mother, I need to say something to you – well, to ask your advice really," Brenda said nervously.

"Of course love, what is it?" Mother asked.

"Well, it's something I have been thinking about for quite some time now, about joining the Royal Air Force, like our Edmund did," Brenda said, looking hopefully at her mother.

"I don't know what to say, Brenda. Are you sure about this? It is a big commitment you know, and I don't imagine it's an easy life, especially not for a woman," Mother said with concern.

"I know, Mother, but the way that Edmund used to talk about it, I feel that I would like to give it a try. Not flying like Edmund, but maybe in communications," Brenda said confidently.

"Well, I suppose if you've made your mind up… you are a young woman and it wouldn't be fair for us to stand in your way. I'll talk to your father about it later, don't worry love."

"Thanks Mother, I knew you would understand. I hope that I haven't upset you," Brenda said.

"No, of course not, I'm OK now. Aren't you three girls going out to the cinema? You had better go and get ready, hadn't you?" Mother added smiling.

The girls chatted while they decided what they were going to wear, and Brenda told Sarah and Alice about her decision.

"Have you spoken to Mother and Father about all this, and are you sure, Brenda?" Sarah enquired.

"Yes, I have given it a lot of thought, and I feel it is what I want to do with my life," Brenda said with conviction.

"Well, that will only leave Greg and I at home," Alice said.

"Until little Jeremy and Jemima come along, that is," Sarah said laughing.

"Don't tell me that you have picked names for them already Alice?" Brenda said.

"No, Sarah's only kidding," Alice replied.

"So Brenda, if you do go into the Air Force, you will write to us, won't you?" Sarah asked.

"Yes of course I will, when I get the time, and the same goes for you, Sarah, when you're in Switzerland," Brenda said.

"Come on, let's go and see the film, otherwise we'll be late," Alice interrupted.

"I'm really looking forward to meeting our Edmund's fiancée tomorrow, so that I can ask her about what she thinks of the Air Force," Brenda said enthusiastically.

"As long as you don't interrogate the poor girl," Sarah said laughing.

They all enjoyed their film, and called for chips on the way home, chatting as they strolled along the street towards home. Sarah felt a little sad, as this would probably be the last time that they would be together like this for a while. But they all had come to realise that it was a time for new beginnings and for change and doing different things with their lives. But even so, Sarah knew that their loyalty would remain and they would be constantly in each other's thoughts.

"Cheer up, Sarah. Come on, I'll race you home," Brenda shouted.

"What about Alice?" Sarah shouted back.

"Don't worry about me, I can still race you two any time," Alice said, starting to run down the street.

"Come on Brenda, we can't be beaten by a pregnant woman, we will never hear the end of it!" Sarah said.

They all got to the gate, Sarah was last, but laughed it off in her usual carefree manner. Mother was inside making some supper; the girls just had some cocoa and sat chatting.

"I feel as though I've got indigestion," Alice said.

"Well, unfortunately love you will probably get things like that now that you are expecting," Mother said.

"It's not that, Mother, these two fools have had me racing up the street," Alice said.

"Here, have a mint Alice. What on earth did you do that for Sarah?" Mother asked.

"It was Brenda's bright idea," Sarah said with a grin all over her face.

"Honestly, I don't know what to do with you lot," Mother said, laughing, and she called Father down for supper.

Father sat in his armchair and looked across at his daughters laughing together happily, he felt proud of all of them. "Brenda, is this right that you wish to join the Air Force? Well, I didn't think anyone else could surprise me after everything I've heard lately, but that certainly did take me by surprise, I must say!" Father said, his voice filled with emotion.

"Are you really all right about it, Father?" Brenda asked, looking for some sort of reassurance, as she did quietly value her father's opinion.

The Winds of Change

"If that is what you really want to do love, then your mother and I wish you well. Just think, though, there will be no more having to wait two hours for the bathroom! But I am not sure your colleagues will wait that long!" Father said laughing; he couldn't resist having a joke with Brenda, but he would miss her terribly too. He sat and thought how all his children seemed to be becoming so independent, and it was a strange feeling for him. As a person who didn't adapt very easily to change, it would take him a while to get used to the idea of it. But despite this he knew deep down that his children's happiness was of paramount importance to him and his wife. That's why he could never stand in their way; after all, it was their life! When they left home hopefully they would be equipped with the values and love that they had been shown over the years. And they would find the time to keep in touch and let their parents know how things were doing.

"Come on, we had better call it a day, Harry. We do want to look reasonable when this young lady of Edmund's comes tomorrow," Mother said.

"That's true enough, dear, and you girls don't be up too late now," Father added.

"OK, Pops, we will be up soon," Sarah replied.

The girls chatted a bit more, and then their younger brother Greg returned from the bakery. He had been helping with the stocktaking and cleaning. He smiled at the girls.

"You three are sat there like the three wise monkeys," Greg laughed as a cushion came flying over at him. "Missed, not a very good shot Sarah!" he added.

"I suppose you want a cup of tea? You always time it right for that kettle! I'll make it," Sarah said smiling.

"Have you heard Brenda's news, Greg?" Alice asked.

"Yes, she told me and I think it's great, and I have some good news myself; I have been promoted to manager at the bakery. The boss told me tonight," Gregory said happily.

"I thought that you seemed more cheeky than usual when you came in, that's great, Greg. Mother and Father have only just gone up to bed, you'll have to go up and tell them your news," Sarah added.

Sarah felt really pleased for Greg, as she knew how hard he had been working at the bakery. He definitely deserved promotion. Everything seemed to be falling into place for all of her family, including herself, and one of the good things that would come of it would be a bit more money around. Life wouldn't be as much of a struggle as it had been for them in the past. She would still continue to send some money home, and Brenda would too. So every bit would help their parents especially when Alice's babies were born.

After their cup of tea they all went to bed on a very happy note and had a good night's sleep.

Sarah awoke the next morning to heavy rain and realised she had slept till nine thirty. She looked round the bedroom to find Alice still sleeping. Gregory and Brenda had gone to work. Alice had a day off to have a bit of a rest. Poor Alice, she wouldn't be relishing the idea of people getting to know about her pregnancy at work. She didn't want to be the subject of their gossip, but she knew that the novelty would wear off after a while And then they would be tearing someone else's character apart. Alice was glad she had always kept herself to herself and never went in for idle gossip. It would never change there at the colliery; it had always been that way. People became "case hardened" in order to carry on working there. But with the likes of Jimmy Thompson and his father working there and on her side, it could only be a bonus for Alice. They were the ones to definitely put anyone in their place who dared to antagonise her, never mind what her father would have to say.

"I am just going to go out and get a few groceries for Mother, I will be back soon," Sarah said. "When I get back we'll have a chat – you know you needn't worry, Alice, there's plenty of time to tell them at work about your pregnancy."

It was just like Sarah. Alice felt so lucky to have her as an older sister. She always had a smile and positive words, no matter what the situation. And in a crisis Sarah seemed to be a tower of strength just when it was needed most. Alice often thought that Sarah took after their mother, with her strength and determination to see things through no matter what. Alice didn't exactly think of herself as a pushover, but she admired Sarah very much and often wished that she could be more like her sister.

Alice put the kettle on and was looking for some biscuits – that was if there were any left by now. When Mother did any baking, everything was soon eaten up.

Suddenly there was a knock on the door. Alice wondered if it was Sarah up to her usual tricks, messing about. She often did that. "Sarah, stop messing about and come in," Alice shouted. But instead of this, when Alice opened the door a lady who she had never seen before stood there looking wet holding an umbrella.

"Oh, I am so sorry, I thought that you were my older sister playing the fool. Do come inside out of the rain," Alice said, feeling foolish herself.

"That's OK, my name is Sally, Sally Whittaker. I am Edmund's fiancée." She smiled nervously.

"Could I take your raincoat, Sally? And I'll make us a cup of tea, it's so nice to meet you at last," Alice replied.

Alice slipped into the kitchen, and Sarah came racing through the door "I'm absolutely drenched) The things I do for parents honestly!"

Sarah turned and noticing the lady sat on the sofa, she said "Oh hello there, I am Sarah, you must be Sally. Pleased to meet you,"

"Hello Sarah, I have heard so much about all of you from Edmund," Sally said.

"Well, we have all been looking forward to meeting you, and how are you? Well I hope?" Sarah enquired.

"I am not so bad under the circumstances. And of course you know about the baby, don't you? At least I feel like I still have a part of Edmund with me. I loved him so very much," Sally replied emotionally.

"I'm sure you did, and I know how much he thought of you. I am only sorry about the circumstances of our meeting," Sarah said regretfully.

"Your sister Alice is making us some tea," Sally said, smiling.

"Will you excuse me, Sally, while I just go and see if she needs a hand?" Sarah added.

As Sarah went into the kitchen she found Alice on the floor looking really frightened. "Sarah, I think it's the babies, can you get me an ambulance? I'm in so much pain!" Alice pleaded. She started to sob as she squeezed Sarah's hand tightly.

"Don't worry, Alice, we will get you to hospital as quick as we can. Mother and I will be with you," Sarah said, trying her best to comfort Alice.

Sarah apologised to Sally and explained that they would have to take Alice to the hospital. Sarah called upstairs to her mother. "Quickly Mother, I need you to come downstairs right away. It's Alice, she isn't too good at all, we will need to take her to hospital. And Sally is waiting down here to see us," Sarah said nervously. Mother came rushing down the stairs.

"Oh Sally, I am so sorry about this, it is so nice to meet you. I'm afraid that Sarah and I will have to go the hospital with Alice. Please stay, as Father will be down in a minute. And I know that Gregory and Brenda are looking forward to meeting you as well. Father will keep you company till we return, if that's OK with you," Mother said anxiously.

"That's fine, and I hope that Alice is OK," Sally added with concern.

"Oh, and Sally, could you please tell Father that we will phone him later and tell him how Alice is?" Mother said as they went out the door.

"I will, and try not to worry," Sally replied.

The ambulance came and took them to the hospital, and as they came through the main entrance, Alice whispered to Sarah, "I want Jimmy to come and see me, will you phone him up for me Sarah please?"

"Of course I will," Sarah said, giving her a kiss on the cheek.

Afterwards, when they were in the waiting room anxiously waiting for news of Alice, Sarah kept thinking about the last time that they were in this same hospital and Father had suffered a heart attack. She hoped that Alice was going to be all right; Sarah couldn't seem to get that terrified look on Alice's face out of her mind.

"I'll get us some tea, Mother, shall I?" Sarah asked wanting to do something as hospitals always tended to make her somewhat nervous. She didn't really know why.

"Could you just stay with me, Sarah, till we find out how Alice is?" Mother said anxiously.

"Of course, I don't mind Mother. I'm sure that someone will come and tell us very soon," said Sarah reassuringly. They waited half an hour before a nurse came to see them.

"Are you related to Alice Watkins?" the nurse enquired.

"Yes, I am her mother, and this is her sister."

"Well, I am afraid that she has had a miscarriage, we lost the baby girl but managed to save the boy. I'm so sorry. We will have to keep her in hospital for a few days, for complete bed rest. Doctor says that if she rests and takes care of herself the other pregnancy should be all right," the nurse added.

"Thank you nurse, could we just see her for a few minutes, then we will go home?" Mother asked.

"Only for a few minutes, as we have given her something to help her to sleep," the nurse replied. As they were going down the corridor to see Alice, Jimmy came rushing towards them.

"How did you know about Alice, Jimmy? I was going to phone you," Sarah said.

"Your father called me at work. It was strange really because he never usually speaks to me if he can help it. But never mind about that, how is Alice?" Jimmy asked.

"I'm so sorry Jimmy, she has had a miscarriage, they lost your daughter but managed to save your son," Mother said with tears in her eyes. She felt so drained and so sorry for this poor young lad.

"Can I see her?" Jimmy pleaded anxiously.

"Of course you can, come with us. They have given her something to sleep but the nurse said we can see her for a short while. And the doctor has said that if she rests in hospital for a few days, hopefully she should be all right," said Mother, trying to reassure Jimmy.

"I know that doesn't make up for losing your baby girl, but the doctor said she was lucky that she didn't lose both babies," Sarah said.

"Sarah, could you go and get us those cups of tea now please?" Mother asked.

"Do you want one as well, Jimmy?" Sarah asked.

"Yes thanks, Sarah," Jimmy answered.

They reached Alice's bed. She lay there looking extremely pale and very tired. She looked up at her mother and said, "I've been waiting for you, no one has told me anything properly yet. What is going on?" Alice asked nervously.

"I'm so sorry sweetheart, we've lost one of the babies, it was a girl. But they managed to save the other baby, it is a boy, Alice," Jimmy said, trying hard not to break down in front of Alice, he cared about her so much.

"I'm sorry, Jimmy," Alice said emotionally.

"Don't you apologise, none of this is your fault at all! I don't want to hear you say that again Alice, it's one of those things that none of us can do anything about," Jimmy answered, doing his best to put on a brave face, but really inside he was heartbroken.

"Please don't go upsetting yourself, love, you must try and get some rest now and we will see you tomorrow, I promise," Mother said.

"Where is Sarah?" Alice asked.

"Don't worry, she has just gone for some tea," Jimmy said.

Sarah came back along the corridor carrying some cups. "Wretched machine! It ran out after two cups, and I couldn't find anyone around. Never mind, you two have these and I'll have a quick word with Alice. Then we must get back to Father and Sally," Sarah said.

"Who is Sally?" Jimmy asked Mother.

"She is our Edmund's fiancée, and she had arranged to come and see us today. And then we had to leave the poor girl as all this happened with Alice," Mother replied.

"Yes, and by now I bet Father has shown her all the family photographs – he's always doing that!" Sarah said laughing.

"I've got my car outside, would you like a lift home?" Jimmy asked them both. "Thank you, Jimmy, that's very kind of you to offer, yes we would," said Mother.

Sarah and Mother sat in the back of the car. It was a quiet journey as no one really felt like conversation as what had happened was beginning to sink in, and they were all feeling the effects from it.

When they arrived home, Mother asked Jimmy if he would like to come in for a minute and have a cup of tea, but he made his apologies, and said he had to go back to work. No doubt everybody would want to know what was going on. Well one thing was for sure; they wouldn't find out anything from him. It was personal, and as far as he was concerned, they could draw their own conclusions on the matter! Jimmy had far more important things on his mind right now than idle gossip. He was going to take good care of Alice when she was able to come out of hospital. No one was going to upset her, and he would make sure that she got proper rest.

Jimmy loved her so much. He just knew that he couldn't bear anything else to happen to her, or the baby. He walked back into work and heads turned as he went through the colliery and into his office. He went to his desk and sat staring out of the window.

Jimmy's boss, Mr Bartholomew, a middle-aged, portly man, put his head round the office door and said, "Are you OK Jimmy? Is there anything I can do?"

"No thank you sir, it's a rather personal matter. I will just get on with my work now. I can make up the time tomorrow, if that's all right with you sir?" Jimmy said.

"Of course, Jimmy, don't worry. I have been very pleased with your work lately," Mr Bartholomew said smiling.

"Thank you sir," Jimmy replied. He continued with his paperwork as best he could, and the afternoon passed quicker than he thought it would. As he was leaving work later, his father shouted out to him, "Are you all right son? And how is Alice? Is she going to be OK?"

"I hope so, Dad. They are going to keep her in the hospital for a few days' rest. She has lost one of the babies, so she will have to take it easy when she comes home," Jimmy added with concern.

"I am so sorry son. But you know she is in the best place at the moment, the doctors will take good care of her. What a shame, she is such a nice girl, especially considering the father she has got! He really is an awkward devil."

"Don't start all that again, Dad. You two are going to have to try and get along, once and for all, even if it's only for mine and Alice's sake, please Dad!" Jimmy pleaded.

"It's not going to be easy Jimmy, but under the circumstances I will try, if you can get him to as well," Jimmy's father said defensively.

"Dad, you sound like you're in the playground! You really need to make the effort if Alice and I are going to have any kind of future together. You do like Alice, don't you Dad?" Jimmy asked emotionally.

"You know I do. I must admit it was a bit of a shock for your mother and me about the babies, but I expect it was just as much of a shock for Alice's parents. But your mum and I are coming round to things," he said.

"Well then, can you promise me, Dad, that next time you see Harry Watkins at work you will at least try to manage a smile?" Jimmy said

"OK!" his father replied, somewhat reluctantly. And then added, "Do you know how he is going on, Jimmy? He had some sort of heart attack didn't he?"

"He's not too bad now Dad, and I think he will be coming back to work next week on light duties," Jimmy said.

"Oh, right then. So we had better get ourselves home, you know what your mother is like if she's cooked a meal and we're not there to eat it," Jimmy's dad said.

When they arrived home Jimmy's mother, Helen, was on the telephone. "Hello you two, I won't be a minute, just put the kettle on Harry, will you?" she asked.

"OK love. Who are you chatting to?" he whispered to her as he went past into the kitchen.

"So she is quite comfortable now, is she? And would it be all right if I sent some flowers to the ward? Thank you I'll just write that down... Thank you, goodbye.

"Right, I will get your meal now. I was just finding out how Alice was."

"That's nice of you Mum, I'm sure that Alice will appreciate that. I said that I would go up to see her again after tea. There is visiting till eight o'clock," Jimmy added.

"Well, give her our love, son, and I hope she's OK. I'm sure the doctors are looking after her, but it must have been frightening for her all the same," his mother said.

"She was very scared, we all were for a while, but hopefully now with plenty of rest she will be OK," Jimmy replied.

They had their meal. Jimmy got ready to go up to the hospital. He put some chocolates in the car for Alice, and set off as he was giving his dad a lift to his darts night. He played for a local team and the club was on the way to the hospital.

"See you later then, son. Give Alice our best wishes," his father said as he got out of the car.

"I will. Can you tell Mum I've got my key? I'll be back late as I said I would call in at Alice's house, after the hospital," Jimmy said.

"What for?" his father asked.

"Because they have invited me for some supper and to meet Alice's brother and sisters," Jimmy added defensively.

"Oh, watch it doesn't turn into the Spanish Inquisition with her father there," his father said grinning.

"There you go again, Dad! Just don't do it!" Jimmy answered angrily.

"I'm sorry, son. Take care, see you later," he said.

Jimmy drove off to the hospital. When he arrived Alice was sat up in bed eating some dinner and looking a little better.

"How are you, love?" Jimmy asked with concern.

"I'm not too bad thanks sweetheart, but I can't wait to get home and back to my job and secretarial course," Alice replied.

"Not so fast, love, you know that you will have to take it easy for a while, Alice, and after everything that's happened to you, I just want to take care of you and make sure you are all right," Jimmy added protectively.

"I know, Jimmy, but even the doctors have said that when I do go home I have to try and carry on as normal; after all, it is a natural thing, pregnancy," Alice said.

"I can see that, just as long as you don't overdo things and wear yourself out at home," Jimmy replied sternly. "Have they said when you can go home yet? I will get the day off work and collect you in the car," he said.

"They have told me I can't go home for another week. I should think I will be bored out of my mind by then," Alice replied tearfully.

"The doctors know best love, they're taking good care of you; that's the main thing, and in the meantime I have brought you some of your favourite chocolates," Jimmy added, smiling.

"Oh, now you are spoiling me. Are we going to have some of them now?" Alice asked, smiling back at Jimmy. She really did love him so much.

"I don't see why not, as long as I can have some of the strawberry creams," he said, laughing and grabbing hold of the box.

"Well, this is all right, you two sat eating chocolates! Are there any left for me?" Sarah asked cheekily as she walked up to the bed with Mother.

"Who bought you those, Alice?" Mother asked.

"Jimmy brought them with him, he's a diamond really, he knows they're my favourite," Alice said.

"He's spoiling you, isn't he?" Sarah said jokingly laughing.

"I've already told him that," Alice replied.

They were all sat chatting and enjoying one another's company when Sarah said, "Have you remembered that it's my going away party tomorrow Alice?"

"Oh goodness, hasn't that come round quick? I still can't believe that you are going," Alice said emotionally.

"Don't you worry about anything because we are going to bring the party to you in hospital so you don't miss out on any of it," Sarah added, feeling so relived that her sister was going to be all right.

"You think of everything, sis. I'm going to miss you so much," Alice said.

"I know, and I will miss you too, but I think that this chap of yours will look after you for me, and we must keep in touch," Sarah replied, her voice filled with emotion.

"And am I going to get to meet this gentleman that's sweeping you off to Switzerland?" Alice asked.

"Of course. He is going to come to the hospital with us tomorrow, so you'll just have to wait till then, won't you," Sarah added grinning cheekily at her sister.

Sarah smiled at Alice, it was good to see her sister looking so much better. She had given her a real scare when they brought her into the hospital, and because of what had happened, Sarah had been able to see for herself how Jimmy truly cared for Alice, and it reassured her somewhat about having to go away.

They decided to go home as Alice was beginning to get tired. They would be back tomorrow evening. Mother also needed to get home to finish off the preparations for the party. She hoped that everything was going to be OK, and she was going to miss Sarah. She hoped that life would be kind to her and the future would be happy for her and Edward. She admired her daughter so much in a lot of ways, especially the fact that she was prepared to go off to a strange country and start a new relationship and a whole new life! It took a special kind of person to even consider doing such a thing. She knew she could never have done that.

Everyone had put their money together to buy Sarah some luggage. Sarah's mother felt sure she would be pleased with her presents.

So much had happened to their family over the past few months, including the tragedy of Edmund's sudden death, touching them all in different ways. As their mother she felt for all her children as different things were beginning to happen in their lives, and as much as she loved them all, there would be times when life would be hard for them and difficult to handle, and she wouldn't always be able to make things better for them as she had done when they were little. That saddened her in a way as she had built her entire life around her children and her husband. Sadly that was one of the harsh realities of life. But she could try to be there for them as much as possible, with advice if needed and constant reassurance.

Sarah found it hard to get off to sleep that evening, everything was going around in her head and certain things didn't seem to feel right, no matter how much she tried to convince herself!

That afternoon she had gone to the Royal Air Force recruitment office with Brenda and watched as her sister talked to the staff and filled in forms. She was so sure that was what she wanted to do with her life. Why couldn't Sarah feel excited and sure about her plans in the way Brenda was? It was no use; she had been trying so hard to convince herself and everyone else around her that she was so happy about going to start this new life with Edward, but it wasn't going to work, she knew that now. The hard part was going to be breaking it to Edward. Poor Edward! Sarah was very fond of him but no matter how she tried she would not be able to love him, especially the way he obviously loved her.

She had to tell him. She couldn't possibly go to Switzerland with him, otherwise she would be living a lie and she couldn't do that, not when Sarah's mother had always told them all to be true to themselves. In the morning she must let Edward know, and not put him through anything else; he would be very upset, but Sarah had to tell him now and not allow things to continue, as she knew it would be for the best in the long run. Neither of them would gain anything by staying together when they both didn't feel the same way.

Sleep came eventually, as she lay exhausted. But the morning brought with it the realisation of what she must face up to.

When Sarah had washed and changed she wandered downstairs. Everyone else had been up for a while and sat eating breakfast. She poured herself a cup of tea. Her thoughts were elsewhere.

"Sarah, be careful love, your tea is running into the saucer," her mother said.

"Oh sorry, I am miles away this morning Mother," Sarah replied.

"I can see that. This is after all an exciting day for you, and to think tomorrow you will be on that plane to a new life," her mother said, trying hard to put her own feelings aside and be happy for her daughter.

"Mother, I can't, you don't understand, I just cannot do this!" Sarah cried as she ran upstairs.

"Whatever is all of this about? Do any of you know what's wrong with her?" Mother asked the others.

Brenda suddenly said, "I think I have an idea, Mother. I don't think she feels able to go through with all this now."

"But why? I thought she had made her mind up, and Edward seems such a nice young man too, whatever will he say about all this I wonder?" Mother said anxiously.

"But surely, Mother, if Sarah is not absolutely certain, then it is better to call things off now than go ahead with her plans and cause upset later on," Brenda said.

Mother was surprised. Brenda was perhaps growing up a little too. There was no doubt in Alice's mind about how she felt about Jimmy, whereas Sarah, on the other hand, after having had time to think things over, had some serious doubts. She had always felt that if she were to meet "someone special" she would really want to feel something strong for that person. Sarah just knew that this was not the way she felt for Edward. It was sad but true.

"Sweetheart, tell me what's wrong. Are you having second thoughts, is our Brenda right about this?" Mother said with concern.

"Yes, I'm sorry but I just can't see things working out. I'm not the one for Edward, and I must tell him so, it is only fair, Mother," Sarah said anxiously.

"Of course, if that's what you really feel, Sarah, then you must tell him, he will respect you for it in the long run," Mother said, trying to support her daughter's wishes.

Sarah began to cry, she had been confused for so long, and now she felt a sense of relief in the midst of all these mixed-up feelings. She knew that deep down it was the right thing to do. Sarah couldn't just tell him over the phone, that wouldn't be right; she owed him an explanation face to face; it was the least she could do.

"You know I will help you in any way I can, Sarah," her mother said with concern.

"I know you will, thanks. I do appreciate it, Mother," Sarah added tearfully. She wiped her eyes and decided she would call Edward up and arrange to meet him that morning.

"I'm so sorry about the party and everything Mother, and all the trouble you have gone to," Sarah added regretfully.

"Never mind about that, all that food will get eaten no doubt. At the moment I am more concerned about you," said Mother.

"I will be OK, I just have to be totally honest with Edward, then maybe I can start to rebuild my life again, making my own decisions," said Sarah.

It was going to be a hard situation for her daughter, but she was the only one who could sort this out. Mother would be there for her if Sarah needed her, and knowing that made all the difference.

Sarah hardly touched her breakfast, and sat with a lukewarm cup of tea, trying once again to find the right words to say to Edward. She had never wanted to hurt him; he was a fine man and a good friend. But she had to be cruel to be kind, as they said. They would both get over it in time.

Sarah picked up the phone. "Is Sadie there pleas? Could I speak to her?"

Sadie was one of the girls Jenny and she had met at the local dance when they were working at the Manor. That seemed a lifetime away now for Sarah. Sadie had a good sense of fun, just the kind of company that Sarah needed right now. Sarah needed to ask her a favour; she hoped that Sadie would be able to help her.

"Hello Sarah, how are you now? I was so sorry to hear about your brother," Sadie said.

"I'm not too bad thank you. I really need to ask you something. Well, my plans for Switzerland have fallen through – it's a long story really which I will tell you later – but I was wondering if I could possibly come and stay with you in your flat? I have some savings for now till I get another position, and we could share the bills. What do you say?" Sarah asked.

There were a few minutes' silence at the other end of the phone. Sarah had a sinking feeling, fearing that Sadie wouldn't be able to help her.

"I think that will be OK Sarah, that's what friends are for after all. When do you want to come?" Sadie asked.

"Could I possibly come tomorrow. There is no point staying here any longer, if that's all right with you, Sadie?" Sarah replied.

"That'll be OK I'm sure. Give me a ring when you are on your way, if you phone at work I'll try and get off a bit earlier. Bye for now then, Sarah," Sadie said.

"Thanks so much Sadie, I really appreciate this. We will have some fun together as well. Bye then," Sarah replied.

Sarah put down the phone and then thought about what she was going to say to Edward. She wished it didn't have to be this way, but it was one of those things; so much had changed in her life recently – mostly things beyond her control. How she missed Edmund! What she wouldn't give to be able to talk to him right now, but the harsh reality was that she couldn't and she would have to face Edward on her own; she could not hide behind anyone else.

She dialled the number, her stomach in a knot. She nervously waited for someone to answer. It was a lady's voice.

"Could I possibly speak to Edward, if he's there?" Sarah asked, a little nervously.

"I'm afraid he isn't. Can I take a message, its his fiancée Gwendolyn speaking?" she said rather abruptly. Sarah froze. She couldn't believe what she had just heard. How could Edward have deceived her in this way? She felt so cheated, and so angry! Tears ran down her face, she never would have believed that Edward of all people could have turned out to be so heartless!

"Yes, there is a message! Tell him Sarah says she is not going to Switzerland with him, and furthermore she never wants to see him again!"

"What – who are you? And what is that supposed to mean?" Gwendolyn shouted.

"Oh, Edward will know exactly who I am!" Sarah snapped, and she put down the phone.

There was she trying to think about Edwards's feelings and hoping to let him down gently, when all the time he had someone else! Although she was absolutely furious, Sarah couldn't help smiling quietly to herself when she thought of this woman. Gwendolyn indeed! She would have liked to be there when Edward returned and Gwendolyn had finished telling him what she thought of him. That would be enough for her, serve him right! Sarah wanted nothing more to do with him. He wasn't even worth her tears. She banged down her fist hard on the table.

"Men! I'm finished with them all, none of them are worth it anyway!" Sarah shouted.

"What on earth's the matter, blossom?" Sarah's father asked.

"Oh Father, where do I start? I had decided not to go with Edward as I didn't really love him like I thought he cared about me, and then I find out that he already has a fiancée no less."

"What, you mean he had another girl all the time he was seeing my daughter?" her father said.

He looked so angry and Sarah was worried about his heart; it wouldn't do his health any good getting in this state.

"Father, if he can do this to me he is not worth you getting worked up over, believe me!"

"I could knock his block off, that's what I could do!" he shouted.

"No, Father, he's just not worth it at all. I've made the right decision for now, I realise that. He's not going to ruin my future, I'm going to stay with a friend, Sadie, in London, till I get myself on my feet again."

"I'm so sorry, love, you don't deserve to be treated this way. It's his loss, you know that, don't you?" her father said sympathetically.

"I do know. Now I need to get on with the rest of my life, and that is why I will be leaving today just the same, only for London."

"Oh Sarah, can't you stay here with us for now?" her father asked.

"No, I'm sorry Father, but I need my independence and to make my own decisions. I will miss you all, but it's something I have to do. I hope you understand. And if that wretch dares to contact me here please don't tell him of my whereabouts, I want nothing to do with him ever again."

"I'm going to miss you, Sarah, but I suppose my consolation is that you are only going to London and not abroad anymore," her father said.

"For the time being, but who knows?" Sarah added.

"Well yes, love, I suppose it's your life, and you must do what you think right," her mother said.

So they all had tea together and said their farewells to Sarah, wishing her luck and happiness in whatever she decided to do. Then Sarah left for the hospital to say her goodbyes to Alice and Jimmy. Alice was going to be surprised at her change of plan, Sarah could still hardly believe it herself! When she arrived in the ward she could hear Jimmy's voice and two other people who she didn't recognise.

"Hello there, how are you today kid?" Sarah asked.

"Oh, not too bad now, the doctors say I can go home tomorrow if everything's OK. Sarah, I'd like you to meet Jimmy's parents, Harry and Helen Thompson," Alice said.

"Pleased to meet you," Sarah said.

"Well, where is your gentleman? You have kept me waiting long enough to meet him anyway," Alice said cheekily.

"Just leave it will you sis? I don't want to talk about it just now," Sarah said quietly.

"But you said you would both be in to see me, I don't bite, what's wrong, he's never shy is he?" Alice said, teasing her sister.

"Just leave it alone," Sarah said, crying.

"Maybe we should go, Alice love, we have been here a while. We will see you tomorrow," Jimmy's parents said, feeling a little awkward in the situation.

"OK, I'll see you tomorrow then, thank you for the fruit," Alice said.

Jimmy said that he would walk them to the door and get himself a cup of coffee so they could talk alone.

"I'm sorry about that, Alice. Please apologise to Jimmy's parents for me, you know I don't usually get upset in front of anyone else," Sarah said, wiping her eyes.

"Whatever's happened Sarah? Where is Edward? Is he hurt or something?" Alice asked with concern.

"I don't think so, but he may well be when Gwendolyn gets hold of him," Sarah said.

"Who on earth's Gwendolyn, and what has she got to do with anything?" Alice asked, wondering what was going on.

"Well, I had decided not to go with Edward to Switzerland as I knew deep down I didn't feel the same way about him, so I phoned up to speak to him and his fiancée Gwendolyn answered the phone," Sarah said angrily.

"I don't believe it! I know I didn't meet him but he sounded so nice, how could he do that to you?" Alice said, feeling so sorry for her sister; she didn't deserve to be treated like that.

"I've been asking myself the same thing, Alice. How could I have been taken in by him like this? I have found out just in time what a bounder he really is!" Sarah said.

"Never you mind, you're worth ten of him, so the question is, what are you going to do now then?" Alice asked.

"I've contacted a friend, and she and I are going to share accommodation for now in London. I have a bit of money saved up that will tide me over until I get another position. When I get settled I will write and give you my address. You make sure that Jimmy takes good care of you and the baby," Sarah said with tears in her eyes.

"Please don't cry again, Sarah, or you will start me off. You look after yourself, won't you? We are all going to miss you, you know," Alice added.

"And I'll miss you too. Mother sent you some goodies from the party. You can eat them later. Now I'll have to be going to catch my bus to the station," Sarah said.

"Jimmy will give you a lift to the station, I'm sure he won't mind," Alice said.

"Here he is now," Sarah said.

"Are you OK, Sarah?" Jimmy asked.

"I'm all right now, but I need to go to get to the station. It's a long story; I'm going to London now instead of Switzerland," Sarah said.

"Oh!" Jimmy said, not really knowing what to say. He didn't really want to put his foot in it. He had seen Sarah upset and thought it best to leave well alone, as she and Alice would have talked it all through while he was out of the ward.

"So do you need a lift then?" Jimmy asked quietly.

"Thanks, that would be good of you," Sarah said, raising a slight smile. "Well, bye sis." She hugged her sister and hoped that the future would be kind to Alice as well as to her own life.

Sarah felt a little nervous, but one thing she *did* know was that any decisions from now on would be made by her alone!

Sarah got into the car and waved to her sister through the window until she was out of sight. Alice had looked so young to be a mother and a little fragile too. Sarah hoped she would be OK. Sarah didn't really know what the future had in store for her, but the winds of change had blown into her life, and nothing would ever be quite the same again.

Printed in the United Kingdom
by Lightning Source UK Ltd.
112560UKS00001B/294